I WANT MY LIFE BACK!

Safwat Alani

ISBN-10: 0615546188
ISBN-13: 978-0615546186

DEDICATION

My love to my mother, who nurtured my fantasy with her vivacious lively "grandma's stories and to my father, who taught and encouraged me in my early years to read poems and literature. To all my family, who tolerated and supported me throughout my life.

ACKNOWLEDGMENTS

To my daughter Sophie and my son Ibrahim, who both worked intensely on formatting the manuscript and on designing the book cover.

= CHAPTER 1 =

Tom Wells cruised along the Interstate in his old Lexus, heading back to his home in a Philadelphia suburb. It was a dull day, with intermittent bursts of rain, and there were some darker storm clouds on the horizon. The windshield wipers were slapping silently, and as intermittent as the rain. Traffic was doing its usual ten miles over the speed limit, Tom's radar detector hadn't been tripped since hitting the Interstate, but Tom still went with the flow. Another hour and he would be home.

Tom had some cause for satisfaction. The client meeting had gone well, and he was expecting more business from it. Management consulting could be a lucrative occupation, and he was getting quite proficient at building his up because, truth be told, Tom was good at what he did.

He glanced at the car clock. Six-fifteen. He should be home by about seven. Chances were though, his wife Jessica wouldn't be there. She would likely be across town at her younger sister Angela's, helping Angela cope with a difficult pregnancy. As soon as that thought came into his mind, Tom was flooded with images from the busy and tragic events of the past few months. The first thing he really felt, though, was a pang of disappointment about going home again to an empty house. It had been happening too often over the last few months, but when he tried to talk to Jessica about it, she would just say that Angela needed her and that ended the discussion. He couldn't deny that Angela did need her sister, Tom's wife. He felt sorry for his sister-in-law. Her husband, a pilot for an international airline, had been killed in a crash only three months ago, when Angela was barely two months pregnant. They had been married less than a year. The shock of her husband's death had put Angela's pregnancy in danger; she was admitted to the hospital for several weeks. After she was discharged, Jessica seemed to spend almost all her time with Angela, helping her through her grief.

Jessica had asked Angela to move in with them for a while in order to forget the pain of losing her husband. Angela seemed pleased at the invitation and Tom had no objections. He knew that Jessica enjoyed Angela's company. They had always been close and had gotten even closer following the death of their mother. Underlying the closeness,

Jessica told him, was a kind of rivalry. The sisters were competitive--always had been, whether it was in track races at high school, in which Angela, two years younger but more gifted athletically, had held her own against her sister, or when it came to dating, and who was dating the cuter guy. Usually any overt jealousy was nipped in the bud. They just got on too well to quarrel for long. Except for one time when they had almost come to blows over who was going to date the captain of the football team.

During her stay at Tom and Jessica's, Angela seemed to recover some of her old spirit. Jessica said it was just like the way it was between them before they had married their respective husbands--Jessica marrying two years earlier than Angela.

The two had amused themselves by going out together taking photographs. That was when they weren't watching and feeling the fetus moving and kicking in Angela's abdomen. Photography was Jessica's main hobby and she pursued it with a passion. When she had married Tom she had insisted that she did not want to work, but wanted the time to pursue her interests of photography and art history. She wanted to build an art collection, which was fine with Tom as long as she didn't break the bank in doing so.

At first during Angela's recovery, Tom had been happy to take a back seat. It seemed only reasonable. And he went out of his way to be friendly and tender to Angela during her stay with them. He was sometimes even quicker than Jessica to fetch Angela something she wanted. Angela joked about what Tom would be like when Jessica became pregnant. Which had not yet happened, in three years of marriage, even though both of them would have been happy to have a child.

Jessica had talked about having a baby at the same time as her sister. They talked about how it would be for the two cousins growing up together, but it wasn't to be, at least not now. Maybe not ever, but no one said anything.

* * *

After some weeks, Angela felt she was stable enough to move back to her own house across town. Her husband had had the foresight to purchase life insurance, and the airline had a separate policy for just such circumstances, so Angela could at least for the time being, afford to live on her own.

After that, it seemed to Tom as if Jessica was with Angela almost every day, helping her in doing everything. That was where Tom's dissatisfaction began to creep in. At first he denied it, telling himself he was being selfish, insensitive, yet... He loved Jessica intensely--he had done so virtually from their first date over four years ago--and wanted her beside him when he came home in the evening. He felt she ought to be there, and he could sense Jessica stiffen a little when finally he couldn't help himself and he made his views plain.

"Angela needs someone to take care of her," she explained again and again. "She needs someone to talk to." Tom felt wearied by it, because he knew Jessica was right, and he could hardly fault her for her concern for her sister. But still he felt a bit cheated and resentful. He wanted Jessica there when he came home; it was as simple as that. He thought that was the deal they had—he earned the money, she stayed at home, took care of the house and enjoyed herself in her spare time. "You're lucky it's only her sister," a colleague had joked a few weeks ago. "My wife ran off with her health club instructor." Tom had smiled ruefully.

Perhaps he was making too much of it. Maybe he should call Dr. Laura. Yeah, right!

As he neared the outskirts of the city, he decided to call her, even though he was pretty sure she wouldn't be at home. Whenever he thought of her as he had been doing, he felt a sudden desire to connect with her--to hear her voice, to see if he could make her laugh, just to feel the texture of her being. He really did miss her whenever he went on business trips.

He slowed the car down below the speed limit as he punched out the number. The phone at his home rang several times. He knew there would be one more ring before the answering machine picked up, and he assumed that, just as he expected, Jessica was not at home. Sure enough, the machine clicked on.

Irritated, Tom decided to call Angela's home, since he was sure Jessica would be there. He punched it out quickly. It was Jessica who answered, her voice bright, feminine, alert, but a little hurried.

"Hi, honey," Tom said, pleased to hear her voice at last.

"Hi, darling. Where are you? I was just about out the door--Angela's experiencing some pain; she's due any day now, so I'm going to get some things for her she'll need in the hospital. The doctor said to be ready to take her anytime if the pain returns and persists."

"Oh," said Tom, "okay." He was trying to disguise the disappointment he felt. "I'm nearly home. About another forty minutes. Had a good meeting."

"Well, I'll call you when I get back. Or I'll call from the hospital if I have to take Angela."

Tom was silent for a minute.

"Okay," said Tom finally, though it wasn't really okay. He knew he wouldn't be seeing Jessica until late. At first he felt frustrated, but then wondered whether he should try to feel differently. Driving your pregnant sister to the hospital didn't seem like the sort of thing you could avoid, even if you wanted to. And he didn't need any persuading. When he thought about it, he knew Jessica loved him. Jessica was a woman of deep passions. It went with all that flaming red hair that cascaded down her back. And when they made love--well, the way Jessica made love left him no doubt of how she felt about him. And there was that unexpected incident where Jessica had seemed annoyed at the attention that he was giving to Angela, as if there was something more to it than simple courtesy. He knew she could be jealous. He was careful not to look at any other woman when they were together. But it had seemed odd to him that one time when she had snapped at him over Angela.

These thoughts cheered Tom up as he continued to drive home. He felt reassured. She did love him. All this sisterly concern for Angela wouldn't be such a problem once Angela had given birth and had her attention occupied with her new baby.

The storm clouds were gathering fast and the light was fading as he pulled into his driveway. He hoped Jessica would be alright.

As soon as he got inside he saw a note on the dining room table, in Jessica's flowing handwriting. "Go to the fridge!" it read. Tom went straight to the refrigerator, and what he saw as he opened the door warmed his heart after his long and tiring day. Jessica had prepared a huge chicken salad for him, complete with her fabulous, home-made dressing. There was a note attached to the bowl which said, "Luv u!!!" It was typical Jessica-- she had found a way of reassuring him of her love even while she was spending all that time with Angela. She could make him feel like such a jerk with the smallest of gestures.

After eating the salad, he slumped in an armchair and reached for the remote. Baseball on ESPN, some boxing on Fox, a breaking political scandal on MS.NBC-- none of it interested him much. He finally settled on a made-for-TV movie that caught his interest even though he knew it was a piece of predictable sentimental garbage.

Outside, the rain poured down and lightning lit up the sky. Tom started to doze off. He hoped Jessica would be home soon. He wanted to have her in his arms.

Tom was awakened by the phone ringing. For a moment he did not know where he was or whether it was night or day. He picked up the phone and grunted a "hello."

"Tom? It's Angela. Do you know where Jessica is? She went out to get some things for me ages ago and she's not back yet. I'm worried about her. And the pains are coming back, so I've gotta call the ambulance and get to the hospital."

"I haven't heard from her, I'm sure she's okay. I know there was a storm but she's a safe driver--"

"They were telling people not to go out."

"Maybe she had to shop around to get the stuff you needed. Don't worry about it. Get the ambulance now. Leave her a note to tell her."

Tom wished her good luck and hung up the phone. He felt slightly uneasy about Jessica, but he knew her so well—she would often take ages to shop, insisting on doing price comparisons even on small items, which meant that she would drive around a lot from store to store. Tom used to point out good-humoredly that if he calculated how much she spent on gas by driving around unnecessarily, it would probably come to more than she saved by getting the best price on the items she wanted. Jessica just laughed. She liked to do things her way, at least as far as shopping was concerned. After all, she used to say with that teasing smile of hers, what do men know about shopping? So it was no surprise to Tom that her errands were taking longer than expected.

He glanced at his watch. It was past nine o'clock. Nothing to do but go back to the TV. He was just beginning to surf through the channels when the phone rang again. This time he picked it up quickly. "Yeah," he said.

"May I speak to Mr. Tom Wells, please," a male voice asked.

"Yeah, I'm Tom," he said, ready to hang up on the telemarketer.

"Mr. Wells, this is Officer Dan Gleeman from the Philadelphia police. I regret that I have bad news for you. Your wife Jessica has been involved in a road accident--"

Tom's heart seemed to leap up into his throat. "What do you mean?" he stammered.

"I'm afraid that Jessica is dead."

What happened over the next few minutes Tom could not later recall. He remembered a daze come over him as the officer told him that on the highway in the storm a truck had crossed the center line and hit Jessica's car head on. Jessica had died instantly.

Tom sat down and gazed blankly into space. It could not be. Not his darling Jessica. She was alive only a few minutes ago. She couldn't be dead now. She couldn't. It wasn't possible. That laugh, that smile, that hair, that body, those hands that had prepared the salad, they couldn't just vanish and be no more. How could this be? But it was. Jessica was dead.

Still in a daze, Tom saw Jessica for himself in the mortuary. Her beautiful face was pale but unmarked. His mind still fighting against disbelief, and tears welling from some wounded place inside but not yet ready to fall, he drove rapidly to the hospital. All he could think of was to break the news to Angela. He couldn't be alone in this.

$=$ CHAPTER 2 $=$

Tom called Angela's home but only got the answering machine. Angela must already have been taken by ambulance to the hospital. Tom decided to rush over there as quickly as he could, although he knew he wasn't thinking clearly. Angela would be in no position to absorb the shock of Jessica's death.

The hospital was a twenty-five minute drive away. When he arrived it was well past midnight. He asked the receptionist where he could find Angela. After some delay he was told that he couldn't see her because she was in the operating room. She was in labor, they told him, and it was taking longer than expected. Tom was persistent and got to talk to one of the doctors, who told him that at first they had thought a "Cesarean section" operation would not be necessary, because everything indicated a normal, uncomplicated labor. But suddenly in the middle of labor, for no obvious reason, the process had stopped moving forward. The head of the fetus was strangely disengaged as if it was being pulled back into the pelvis. The doctors diagnosed the condition as an unusual case of inertia of the uterus. First they tried some injections, hoping to promote the labor and initiate the muscular contraction of the uterus again. But when they didn't see a sufficient response, they decided to perform an urgent Cesarean section operation, which was still going on.

There was nothing Tom could do but wait. He felt utterly drained, sick inside, and not knowing what to do. He sat for hours in the waiting room, ignoring the suggestions of the nursing staff that he go home and get some sleep. He just didn't feel capable of initiating any action at all. All he could do was sit, as if he were only half-alive. He knew he should be calling relatives and friends with the terrible news, but he couldn't bring himself to do it.

Then came the news, delivered to him by a pretty nurse in a blue uniform. The operation had been successful. Angela had given birth to a healthy daughter. Mother and baby were doing fine, but Angela was still under sedation and it would be a while before she could see anyone.

It was past four in the morning, and Tom returned home, driving through deserted, quiet streets. He felt exhausted, but he knew that within a few hours he had to start making funeral arrangements and calling relatives and friends. In spite of his exhaustion, he felt a little calmer than earlier, but he could still not believe that Jessica was really gone. When he got home he kept expecting to hear her voice coming from the bedroom, chiding him for coming in so late.

* * *

Tom slept for about two hours. Then he made calls to his parents, a few of his friends, and to Jessica's friends. Jessica's own parents were dead and she had few other relatives. Everyone asked if there was something they could do, but Tom said there was nothing to be done. He would make all the necessary arrangements and would let them know. But now he had to face Angela and tell her the sad news, when she had given birth only hours before. A birth and a death on the same night. It wrenched his heart.

He drove back to the hospital as the morning sun shone down warm. Normally he loved these late-May mornings, but he wondered whether he could ever love one again. He cried silently and kept turning over and over in his mind how he could tell Angela about what had happened. She would probably still be weak from her own ordeal. Just as he approached the hospital, he made his decision. He would not tell her today. He would wait until she had recovered from the birth.

As he entered her room, Angela looked up and gave a weak smile. It was a very different face than Jessica's—more round and with a lighter complexion. Angela's hair was brown, and she kept it fairly short, quite different from Jessica's flame-red hair that always caught people's attention. But Angela, who was a couple of inches taller than Jessica, had her own kind of beauty—quieter, less spectacular--which also meant that she was never short of admirers, even after she had married. Tom felt a genuine affection for her.

"Where's Jessica?" were Angela's first words to him.

"She's coming in later--this was a bit too early for her," he replied, before he even had time to think what he was saying. "I told her about the baby. She was happy to hear the news of course."

"I was worried about her last night."

Tom did not know what to say.

"Your eyes look red—are you sure you're all right?" Angela asked.

"I just got something in my eye on the way over here . . . " Tom began before his voice trailed off. Then he recovered himself. "I should be the one asking you how you are, not the other way round." But his voice lacked conviction.

"Tom, what's wrong? It's Jessica, isn't it? Tell me." Angela sat up in bed, fixing Tom with an intense gaze.

Tom could no longer keep up the pretense. He started to sob as he told Angela about the accident. Once the tears had started he could not control them. The blood had drained from Angela's cheeks and she looked ghostly pale. Tom went over to her and embraced her as she began crying uncontrollably also. "I'm sorry, I'm sorry," Tom kept whispering as he held her. "Jessica was so wonderful. I don't know what I'll do without her."

Finally, Angela lay back in exhaustion. Tears stained her cheeks and she looked frail. Tom wanted to comfort her, and for a few moments he forgot his own grief and felt only compassion for Angela. He might have lost a wife whom he had known for four years, but Angela had lost a sister whom she had known and loved all her life. Her loss was greater. He decided there and then that he would help her through it. He would be there for her.

At that moment a nurse entered the room with the baby girl, whom Angela had decided to call Linda. The nurse looked from Angela to Tom and then back again. It was obvious something was wrong. Tom explained that they had had bereavement and were still in shock over it. The nurse looked concerned; then a tender look came on her face as she handed the baby to Angela.

Angela smiled wanly and took the baby, held it close to her and cried silently. Then gradually her pained expression gave way to a joyous smile. Even in the midst of her grief, her first baby fulfilled the desire of her heart. Then she remembered her beloved Jessie and started crying again.

Graciously she handed the baby to Tom. He felt his eyes go moist again. He couldn't remember when he had last held a newborn, or even if he had ever done so. He cradled baby Linda in his arms and looked down at her. The baby opened her eyes and looked back at him.

"Well, she certainly likes you!" said the nurse, observing this. "A few hours baby can't normally open its eyes."

Tom smiled. Holding the baby made him happy for a moment. How Jessie would have loved to have been here.

After a while he handed the baby back to Angela so she could feed her. He wanted to leave the room at that point, but Angela insisted that he stay. The baby was suckling and her eyes seemed to follow Tom as he paced restlessly around the room. Angela had fallen silent and appeared not to notice that her baby's eyes were fixed on Tom!

Angela stayed a few more days in the hospital. Tom visited her regularly, staying with her and the baby as long as he could. He took four-weeks off from his business so he could take care of all that had to be done in the wake of Jessica's death.

The funeral was a bleak affair, and no one had any explanation of why a young and vibrant life should be cut off so suddenly like that and for no reason at all. It was such a waste, like tossing a beautiful rose into the garbage. Tom's friends tried to comfort him, but he knew it would be a long time before things got back to normal. He could not imagine a time when the memory of Jessica and her death would not cause him grief and loneliness.

But life had to go on, and Angela needed help, so it was clear to Tom where his duty lay. Angela was the only one who was linked to him after Jessica's death. Angela told him that she felt the same towards him.

The new baby created another bond between them. Here was a source of joy in the midst of their loss. And there was no doubt that the baby seemed attached to Tom. Every time he was in the room Linda would open her eyes and look towards him. When he took her in his arms, she looked into his eyes, and he felt a strange feeling that he couldn't explain.

"It's like a magic," Angela said. "When you come in, she opens her eyes!"

* * *

When Angela was ready to leave the maternity hospital, Tom had a long discussion with her.

"I want you to come and stay with me until you're strong enough to take care of Linda alone," he said.

Angela looked doubtful. "I don't want to do that, Tom. It's really kind of you, I totally appreciate it. But I think we should do it the other way round. You should come and stay with me. Your house will just remind me of Jessie. I need time before I can go back there."

"I know. I feel the same. Everything at home reminds me of Jessica. I guess it'll take a while."

They decided that Tom would indeed move temporarily to Angela's, as long as she needed his assistance. He felt as if he was doing Jessica's sister a favor, which Jessica herself would have done, had she been alive.

After her discharge from the hospital, the first thing Angela did was visit the Jessica's grave with Tom. They laid some flowers and stood in silence for a while. There were no words to say.

* * *

At first things went well at Angela's house. Tom and Angela bonded like two people who had survived a great tragedy together. Tom got a lot of fun out of playing with Linda and Angela seemed grateful to have him around. Tom still thought of her as the sister of his wife, so there were no complications to their relationship. They were just good friends, helping each other out, and bound together by their mutual love for Jessica and for baby Linda.

But after a couple of months, cracks began to form in the previously smooth arrangement. Tom started to get tired of going back and forth from Angela's house to his own, where much of his business was conducted. In the wake of Jessica's death he had decided to do less traveling and spend more time working out of his home.

He discussed the matter with Angela. Why didn't they just switch for a while? She could come and live with him rather than the other way round. Tom hated to move back to his house alone, even though Angela no longer needed his help the way she had done at first. She had now recovered her strength and was rapidly learning how to be a perfect mom to her infant daughter. But Tom needed somebody whom he could talk to, someone who would continue to fill the emptiness he still felt. He was glad when Angela agreed to move temporarily. He was surprised when she told him that the house still reminded her of her past, and her deceased husband. What a couple they were, Tom thought ruefully. Each with a house haunted by a dead spouse.

So it was that bit by bit, Angela and Tom began to form a closer bond. Tom noticed how at first Angela seemed to feel embarrassed at staying at his house, as if she were a guest who felt she always had to be saying thank you. He felt touched by that--by her uncertainty, her simple gratitude. He began to think of her not as his wife's sister, but as Angela, a beautiful woman in her own right, someone who fully deserved his deep affection.

Gradually, Angela seemed to relax, and Tom took pleasure in observing how she started to act as if she really was in her own home. He was grateful to her. She was filling up his emptiness with the warmth of her presence, and he hoped and believed that he was doing the same for her. They seemed to perfectly complement each other's lives. And Tom was so attached to Linda that he felt like she was his own daughter. Linda kept following Tom with her eyes, wherever he went. She smiled when he talked to her, and laughed only when he talked to her or played with her. When he was not around, Linda didn't interact with her mother in the same way. Angela mentioned this to Tom, but he didn't attach any importance to it. He thought it was because he was always playing with Linda, while Angela was busy doing other things with the baby, like feeding her, bathing her, or changing diapers. She didn't have time to play with her as much as Tom did.

* * *

After about three months, of this arrangement, Tom suggested to Angela that she stay permanently in his house. She seemed to shrug the suggestion off, not willing to make a commitment. But Tom's feelings for her continued to grow, although that did not mean he had forgotten Jessica. But he could not ignore the deep fondness he felt for Angela.

A few months later, one pleasant late fall Sunday afternoon when it was still just warm enough to sit out for a while on the deck, he proposed marriage. He hadn't really planned to say it there and then; the words just came out, sounding almost casual.

A look of shock and surprise crossed Angela's face and she shook her head.

"Are you just feeling sorry for me?" she asked.

"No, of course not, why should I feel sorry for you? You're doing fine. I said it because it's what I want. I admire you; I'm attracted to you."

"But we're not in love, are we? Not like I was with Mark, or you with Jessie."

"Maybe not--at the moment. But we get along well. And there's Linda. She's used to having us both around, and we both love her, I know that. Love and deeper understanding--between us, I mean--will come with time."

Angela sat back in her chair and said nothing for a few moments. Then she said simply, "I accept, yes, let's get married."

Tom leant forward and kissed her gently. It was the first time they had kissed.

The wedding was a low-key affair. Only a few close friends were invited. This seemed appropriate under the circumstances. Afterwards, there was a small reception at the newly weds' home.

During the party Linda was very upset and restless, crying all the time for no obvious reason. Tom couldn't sit and talk to his guests for long without interruption. He was kept busy looking after Linda, who wouldn't respond to Angela. Linda cried whenever Tom left her alone. Later on that night, when all the guests had gone home, Tom and Angela discovered that Linda had a fever. Concerned, they called for a doctor, who told them that the problem could be a viral infection or due to psychological stress. He couldn't find any sign of a specific disease.

The fever went up and down the whole night. Tom and Angela couldn't relax or make love on their wedding night.

Next morning, Linda had returned to normal. There was no sign of the previous night's illness. She was happy and playful as usual.

= CHAPTER 3 =

The first word Linda said was "Tom"! She didn't say mom or dad. When she first started to crawl, she developed a habit of going to the closet where Jessica's belongings were stored. Whenever Tom and Angela searched after her they would find her there, playing with Jessica's dresses and shoes. Sometimes she talked to herself, and neither Tom nor Angela could understand what she was saying.

One evening, Linda was playing in Jessica's closet as usual. Tom was in the same room, changing his clothes. Then something made him stop and stand still, his shirt unbuttoned. He had just heard a familiar voice, or he thought he had. It sounded like Jessica, and it was coming from the closet.

"I can't find . . ." said the voice again.

Tom felt his heart twist around in sudden dismay. *What the . . . ?* He fairly leapt across the room and tugged the closet door open.

Linda was sitting on the floor of the closet, with Jessica's jewel case open in front of her. Her tiny fingers were busy searching.

"What did you say, Linda?" Tom asked, still astounded.

She shrugged her shoulders and crunched up her mouth a bit.

Tom looked at her and did not know what to say. This was uncanny. That shrug, and the way she reminded him of someone else. And that someone else was his dead wife Jessica.

Linda looked at him with a smile, "No, Tom, no," she said.

Tom was speechless. That was exactly the expression that Jessica used to use, and Linda had said in exactly the same way, with the same inflection of the voice. How could that be?

With trembling hands he took the jewelry from Linda's hands and lifted her out of the closet. He sat on the edge of the bed, his whole body now trembling.

* * *

Angela was optimistic about how her life was developing. She loved being a mother, and she appreciated Tom's kindness and the love he showed her. Perhaps her feelings for him were not as passionate as they had been for her first husband, but she was wise enough to know when she had got a good man. She suspected that Tom did not feel as passionate about her as he had done for Jessica, but she accepted that. Angela and Tom had promised themselves that their love, born out of tragedy, would grow over the years, and Angela was sure that was happening.

Linda was a beautiful little girl, already with a clear resemblance to her mother. She started to talk when she was two years old. Angela was in no doubt that she was a very unusual child. For one thing, Linda insisted on calling Tom and Angela by their names. Angela could not get her to say "mommy" or "daddy." She assumed that Linda had just heard those names spoken a lot and liked to use them.

But there were things about Linda that puzzled Angela. Things that just couldn't be explained. Things that were more than a little eerie.

When Linda was safely asleep, for example, Angela and Tom would take the opportunity to lie in bed flirting or making love. But Linda would always wake up in the middle of their scene and start to cry. This didn't happen if they were doing something else. It was only when she and Tom were making love.

Perhaps it was just coincidence, Angela said to herself. But there were other incidents. Sometimes when Linda woke up crying, she would moan unintelligibly about darkness and storms and rain. Just a bad dream, Angela would assume. After each nightmare, Linda would refuse to go back to sleep in her own bed. She wouldn't calm down until she was sleeping between Angela and Tom. Nothing unusual about that, she supposed, but when Linda went to sleep in that situation, she insisted on holding Tom in a special way, by putting her head on his neck, and once Tom remarked, "That's exactly like Jessica used to do."

The remark had bothered Angela. The truth was that when she was in bed with Tom, she didn't want to be reminded of Jessica.

* * *

Then came Linda's third birthday. Angela and Tom were busy in the kitchen making a birthday cake for her. They heard a voice coming from the bedroom. "Finally, I found it!" the voice shouted. It was Linda, of course, but her voice sounded different and it was a while before Angela could place it. Then she realized. It was Jessica's voice.

Tom had heard it too, and for a moment they looked at each other. Angela was wondering if Tom was thinking the same thought that she was. They both rushed to the bedroom. Inside, Linda was staring at her reflection in the mirror. She was wearing one of Jessica's dresses, which trailed behind her on the floor, and one of Jessica's necklaces. She appeared to be talking to herself and didn't turn her head when Angela and Tom entered the room.

Still looking in the mirror she said, "I couldn't wear it before." Then she turned to Tom, and said, "Don't you think I have good taste, Tom?"

Angela felt herself freezing up inside. This was simply weird. "Why don't you take the dress off, Linda," she said gently, carefully.

Linda ignored her. "Don't you see Tom?" she shouted. "These are mine. I like them. You know that!"

Tom just stood there, mute.

"Okay, you can keep the necklace, darling, but please take the dress off--look, it's too much long for you," said Angela.

This time Linda did as she was told, and the strange atmosphere that had developed in the room evaporated. Linda seemed calm, and readily agreed, at Tom's suggestion, to go into another room and play with some of her dolls. Angela and Tom went back to the kitchen to finish off the cake.

A short while later, the three of them sat down around the kitchen table, on which sat a birthday cake with three candles. Angela still felt tense after the earlier incident. Linda, who was sitting between Angela and Tom, was playing with the medallion of the necklace. She seemed restless and unhappy, as if there was some sadness pressing in upon her. Angela noticed.

"What is it, Linda?" she asked.

"You know my name is not Linda!"

The little girl was shouting, and her face reddened. She looked at Tom and then at Angela. Then she looked away and smiled a faint smile.

Angela felt a strange feeling, a mixture of fear and apprehension.

"What is your name then?" she said, smiling.

Linda didn't answer.

"Can you tell me?" Tom asked, trying to smile to put Linda at ease.

"My name is Jessica," said Linda calmly, looking directly at Tom. "You knew that."

Angela looked across at Tom. Her forehead was creased in a frown. What on earth was Linda talking about? She felt some sort of obscure fear rising up inside her.

Both adults looked intently at Linda. What was this little girl trying to tell them?

"Why did you say that, Linda?" Tom asked.

"I said I'm Jessica, not Linda," Linda replied. This time she spoke more calmly, although all the time she was playing nervously with the necklace and looking out of the window. She would not meet Angela's eye. What sent a bolt of fear through Angela was the fact that Linda's voice really was like a child's version of Jessica's-- the same inflection, the same tone. Angela shivered.

After a few seconds of tense silence, Linda stopped looking out of the window and turned to look at first Tom and then Angela.

"Say something," she said, her child's face looking inquisitive.

Angela had gone numb. Her only thought was to change the subject. She looked at Tom and said, "Tom, can you help Linda blow out the candles?"

A furious voice similar to Jessica's burst out from Linda, "I have just told you I am Jessica. So don't call me Linda anymore."

"All right, all right, Jessica," Tom said firmly, "Are you satisfied now?"

Linda started to cry and she threw her necklace onto the floor. Angela got up from her chair, leaned over, and tried to lift Linda. But Linda pushed Angela away. She was looking at Tom with her eyes full of tears. Then Tom stood up and lifted her up in his arms. She threw her arms around his neck and cried even harder, sobbing about storms, and dusk and rain.

After a few minutes she quieted down and a smile returned to her face. Soon she was sleeping in Tom's arms.

* * *

Later, when Linda was safely in bed, Tom and Angela discussed the incident.

"I think we should see a doctor about her," Angela suggested.

"I don't think we should make a big fuss about it," said Tom.

But Angela was worried. This wasn't the way she wanted to be reminded of her sister. She reminded Tom of Linda's sudden voice changes and her fear of storms, rain, and darkness.

Tom didn't say anything. But they both remembered the circumstances under which Jessica had died, even though they didn't want to discuss it. Eventually Tom agrees that they should have Linda examined by a child psychiatrist.

Two weeks later they drove with Linda into downtown Philadelphia to the offices of the psychiatrist. The psychiatrist, a plump woman in her forties, was satisfied with Linda's intelligence, her level of development for her age and especially her psychological condition.

"She's a healthy little three-year-old, that's what she is," the doctor said. "As far as her fascination with Jessica is concerned, I think she must just have overheard you talking about her, that's all, and the rest was supplied by a very active imagination. She'll forget soon. Don't worry!"

The woman's manner was so confident and reassuring that both Angela and Tom felt relieved. The doctor advised them to put away all the pictures of Jessica and her belongings. "Then put her in kindergarten as soon as possible, to change her atmosphere," she said.

Angela and Tom did as the doctor suggested. Linda was admitted to a nearby kindergarten and the situation improved.

Over the next few months, Linda seemed much more settled and quite. She seemed to have forgotten whatever it was that had been troubling her. The kindergarten kept her busy all day, and when she came home, she was very tired, and so she slept early. There was no more searching after Jessica's belongings. Linda seemed to sleep well, and was not disturbed by bad dreams. Angela and Tom were satisfied.

* * *

On Linda's fourth birthday. Tom was wokcn up in the middle of the night by some noise coming from downstairs. Not wanting to disturb Angela, who always slept more soundly than he did, he got up and sneaked out of the bedroom. He stood and listened. Then he crept downstairs, where he discovered that the noises were coming from the basement, where there were some valuables stored. His next thought scared him--there might be a burglary in progress. He went back upstairs and took his pistol from a drawer in the desk at the far side of the room. He had never fired this gun (or any gun), and Angela had wanted him to get rid of it, but he had not. He had the safety of his family to think about. Now, as he crept back down the stairs, he was glad that he had the gun. He could hear his heart pounding. When he opened the door that led down into the basement, he saw the light was on and he heard voices. He hesitated to go down, wondering whether he should call 911 and let the police deal with it.

But then as he stood there, indecisive, he recognized one of the voices. It was Linda, her child's voice quite distinctive. She was talking to someone else. Fear gripped Tom as he slowly descended the stairs. Was Linda being abducted by another person? But then he recognized the other voice, a voice that he knew so intimately and could never forget. It was Jessica's voice.

Tom stood in the middle of the stairs as if he was pinned to the ground. He was so scared. He slipped the gun back into his pocket.

"I know they forgot everything about me," Jessica's voice said, her tone conveying annoyance.

"Keep quiet, somebody's coming," Linda's voice said.

When Tom reached the foot of the staircase he saw Linda sitting alone on a chair holding a mirror and gazing into it. She was wearing Jessica's dress again. Tom was so frightened, and his heart was beating fast. He remembered that he and Angela had stored all of Jessica's belongings in the basement.

Slowly he walked towards Linda, who glanced at him and then went back to looking in her mirror. Tom felt his mouth was very dry. He couldn't swallow. He didn't know what to say.

Eventually, some words came. "Linda, what are you doing here?" he said quietly. He was shivering.

She looked at him and smiled. Then she repeated his words in a mocking tone, in Jessica's voice, "Linda, what are you doing here?" She shook her head. "Don't you ever learn? You don't understand, Tom. I'll get you! You will see."

Tom just looked at Linda for what seemed like a very long time. This was the most eerie thing he had ever encountered. Thoughts of Jessica came flooding into his mind as he stared at the four-year-old girl dressed in Jessica's clothes and talking the way Jessica talked. His mind went numb. This was beyond his understanding. He was very frightened, too frightened to continue the conversation.

After a minute or so, with a huge effort, Tom blocked out what he was seeing and hearing. She's just an imaginative four-year-old, that's all, he told himself. He knew that wasn't a satisfactory explanation, but it enabled him to take some action. He reached out, took Linda in his arms and made his way upstairs, stumbling at times as his feet got entangled with Jessica's long dress. Linda had gone silent and did not resist. Tom put Linda to bed and then returned to his own bed. Angela was still sleeping.

Tom could not get back to sleep. He lay awake, thinking, wondering about what had happened.

In the morning, he confided in Angela. Perhaps partly because of the bright morning sunlight that streamed into their bedroom, Tom did not feel so anxious or disturbed about it as he had during the night. Strange events seemed less threatening by daylight.

* * *

Over the next few years, every now and then there were similar incidents. Each time they happened, Tom and Angela were both shaken. But they couldn't find a way to prevent Linda from acting both as Jessica and Linda at the same time. Sometimes they would think that Linda had forgotten Jessica completely, but suddenly the little girl was Jessica again--in her voice and gestures and even in her way of thinking. Angela began to accept the fact that Jessica was present. She didn't know how it could possibly have happened, but convinced herself that Jessica wanted to be remembered through Linda. It was a peculiar thing to accept, and there was much about it that disturbed Angela, but she had developed a habit of forgetting about it except when another strange incident took place.

As for Tom, he went further than Angela. He accepted not only the fact that Jessica was somehow present in Linda; he was also convinced that Jessica--his beautiful dead wife--had somehow lived on and had become Linda. Or Linda had become Jessica. He didn't know how to think of it. Thus every time he held the child Linda in his arms he felt like he was holding his Jessica. It was a most peculiar feeling--comforting, but also deeply disturbing to his heart and mind. He couldn't tell anyone about it. Not even Angela.

= CHAPTER 4 =

Ten years passed. Linda was fourteen years old, a freshman in high school and a young woman in body and mind. She seemed to Angela and Tom to be for the most part a well-adjusted girl. Her school grades were usually good, and she seemed to have quite a lot of friends her own age. Recently she had been showing some signs of moodiness and rebelliousness, but Angela and Tom had put this down to her age. What teenage girl or boy couldn't get difficult sometimes? It was natural for youngsters to want to separate themselves from their parents (in this case, mother and stepfather), so Angela, who was the main enforcer of discipline, decided with Tom's approval that they should cut her some slack and not make up too many rules that she would only delight in breaking.

One October evening just before supper Linda was in her room talking on the phone. Tom and Angela were sitting at the dining table waiting for Linda to come down and join them to eat. After a while Angela called her down for a second time.

"*All right!*" yelled Linda, clearly irritated by Angela's insistence that she come and eat her food before it got cold.

A few moments later she ran down the stairs and sat down at the table. She said nothing and looked around the room as if impatient over something.

"Who was that on the phone?" Tom asked.

"My friend," Linda said, sounding very uninterested.

"He or she?"

"She," said Linda, more than a trace of irritation in her voice. "It was Jane. Satisfied? What did you expect?"

"Linda, there's no need to be rude," interjected Angela.

"I'm not being rude."

"I thought you were probably talking to your boyfriend," Tom said, smiling.

"What? My boyfriend?"

"Yes. The boy who always accompanies you home from school."

"That dummy!" Linda laughed. "Do you really think he was my boyfriend?"

"Well, I thought so. It is normal nowadays, dear," Tom said, smiling, wanting to calm her down. "You must have a preferred somebody, some…"

Linda's face suddenly contorted in rage. "I have only you, don't you see?" she burst out, her voice rising. "I had nobody else in this life or…"

She looked fiercely at Tom and then across at Angela, who had stopped eating in dismay. Linda threw her fork down on the table and stormed off upstairs, sobbing.

Angela got up and was about to follow Linda upstairs, but Tom restrained her.

"No, just leave her. She'll calm down."

"Why did you ask her that?" said Angela, reproachfully.

"Well, we've both noticed that lately she's been very quiet and introverted. She stays a lot in her room. I thought she might be depressed."

"So what are you getting at?"

"I thought she might be depressed because of something happening in school. Possibly with her boyfriend."

"But Tom, I know she has no boyfriend."

"How do you know that? And isn't it unusual not to have..."

"You heard her, Tom," Angela interrupted him with firmness. "Do you think she's changed just because she's now fourteen years old? Don't try to convince me that she's forgotten the past."

"What do you mean she hasn't forgotten--forgotten what?"

The two of them had not spoken about this for some while, and Tom didn't want it to come up again. There were so many things swirling in his mind that he didn't want to discuss with Angela.

"Tom, we must face it." Angela was looking directly into his eyes. "Linda is not my daughter. All of us know that. She's my sister, Jessica!"

"Oh, Angela! Come on!" Tom was raising his voice. "She's still a child. I'm sure she'll meet somebody soon, and--"

"What?" Angela shouted. "No, Tom, I don't think so. She is Jessica. She's Jessie in everything she says, does or thinks. You know that. You're just running away from it."

Tom felt a shiver of confusion and despair run through him, but he wasn't prepared to say what he really felt.

"Angela! I'm sure she either has forgotten or will soon forget all that."

"How and when, Tom?" Angela asked sharply. "What do you think she was trying to tell us just now?"

"When she finds the right boyfriend . . ." Tom began but then trailed off. He knew he was trying to convince Angela of what he himself didn't believe.

"You know every daughter looks up to her father in the early years of her life and--"

"Please, Tom," Angela interrupted. "Will you stop it, don't be unrealistic. First, you're not her father. We have to face up to this. I said let's face the truth! She is Jessica in every meaning of the word. She loves you as Jessica did. That's it. Do you understand what I'm trying to tell you? Have you seen the way she looks at you?"

Tom didn't utter a word. He knew that what Angela was saying was the truth. The truth that both of them had tried for years to avoid facing or mentioning. Tom leaned forward, holding his head in his hands. Angela was looking out of the kitchen window with tears filling her eyes.

After a while, Tom asked quietly, as if he was asking himself, "How can you be sure you're right? What are your grounds for believing it?"

"I know it for sure. That's it! Don't ask me how." Angela wiped away tears. "I was hoping like you that it was just a child's story that she'd grow out of. But it hasn't happened."

Tom felt a sudden rush of anger. "Have you been talking to a psychiatrist lately?" he said in a mocking tone. "Or reading some hocus-pocus psychology book?"

"Oh, don't be stupid, Tom. I've been observing Linda, that's all, and I know. Okay?"

Angela couldn't bring herself to tell Tom about why she was so certain of what she was saying. There had been an incident two years ago, when she was cleaning Linda's room. She found a diary hidden under Linda's mattress. When she opened it she was shocked. The book was not the usual kind of diary. Written in Linda's childish hand, it recorded memories of events from her very early childhood, when she was two or three years, which usually nobody could remember about their own lives.

Some photos of Jessica had fallen out from inside the diary. When Angela picked them up, she noticed that on the back of each photo Linda had written some notes. The notes were unbelievable. They described exactly the circumstances in which the photos had been taken. A chill ran through Angela. For a moment the thought that came to her was crystal clear: my sister is somehow alive inside the body of my daughter. She was afraid to read more and stuffed the photos back in the diary and replaced it under the mattress.

On subsequent days, however, Angela went back to the hidden diary and secretly read what Linda had written. She had felt a mixture of shame, guilt and horror in doing so. She was spying on her own daughter, and she was terrified of what she might read. But she did it anyway.

After a few moments of tense silence between them, Tom said, "I don't understand what you are saying! What do you mean?" Deep inside, he feared that he knew exactly what she meant.

"Please, Tom, don't ask me more. Linda believes I betrayed her by marrying you. I took you from her."

"What!" Tom raised his voice.

"Don't raise your voice, please. She feels that I took you from her by marrying you."

"How did you know all these things? Did she tell you that?"

"No, she didn't."

"So, it's all your imagination? Isn't it so?"

"No, Tom! No, it's not my imagination. These are the facts, which she believes."

"Tell me how? How did you know that?"

"I can't tell you . . . now!"

"Why? Why do you make everything mysterious and complicated?"

Angela shook her head. She didn't answer. Barely controlling his frustration, Tom walked away from Angela and headed upstairs to Linda's room. Angela ran after him.

"Please, Tom, don't tell her what I have just told you," she said. "Even if she mentions what I told you, don't tell her that I told you the same. Please."

Tom knocked on Linda's door. There was no reply. He opened the door slowly and entered. He found her lying in her bed.

"Linda! Are you sleeping?"

She didn't answer, and turned her face away. Tom sat down on the edge of the bed, taking her hand in his hand. He didn't say a word. She didn't move.

After a while, Linda spoke. "What do you want from me, Tom?" Linda asked in a small voice, still refusing to look at him.

"I want you to be happy," Tom said, looking at her and making himself smile. "That's all."

"That's all?" Linda asked. "Well, I am happy, OK?"

"That's good to hear." Tom said. "Do you want me to leave?"

"No!" Linda said with a sigh.

"Why don't you turn your face to me then?"

"Because I don't want you to see my ugly face when I'm crying."

"Why do you cry, first of all?" Tom said.

She started to wipe off her tears. "I don't want you to see my ugly face when I'm crying."

"Yes, I know, but Linda, why are you crying?" Tom asked gently. "I'm sorry that I asked you a silly question."

Linda closed her eyes, pursing her lips, when Tom called her Linda.

After a few seconds she said, "No, no, Tom, it wasn't silly. I felt that you was thinking of me and caring for me."

"Of course I'm caring for you," Tom said, smiling. "What do you think?"

"Well, I don't know what to think," Linda said sighing, "or what to hope for in this life." She sounded much older than her fourteen years.

"Why are you so pessimistic, Linda?" Tom said with a soft voice. "You are still at the beginning of your life; you must look forward to the future. I am sure it will be full of nice surprises. Enjoy your life, Linda."

At the mention of her name, Linda turned her face to the wall again. Her eyes were suddenly filled with tears. Tom noticed the sudden reaction, but he didn't understand the reason for it.

"Linda, can you tell me what's wrong?" he asked tenderly.

She turned to him and looked at him with teary eyes. "All right. There's nothing wrong with me." She looked as if she was trying to control herself and not burst out crying. Her eyes were red and the tear stains showed on her cheeks. "But you and Angela always call me Linda, daughter Linda. You know very well I am your Jessica, not Linda. You don't give a damn about what I feel."

"I am very sorry that we had left you suffering like this, without my knowledge," Tom said, that while wiping Linda's tears with his hand. "I couldn't even imagine that you still remember--"

"Because I didn't say a word to you all these years," Linda interrupted him, "you thought that I had forgotten who I am. But I didn't mention anything because I knew both of you were afraid to face it, to face the truth. You were so cowardly you wouldn't admit it. You wanted your life to continue as is, pretending everything is OK, as normal as it should be. You wanted to erase the memory of me and live in a false peace."

She was spitting the words out and was once again close to tears. Tom had never heard Linda speak like this and he had little idea of what to say. And the thought that this adolescent girl in front of him, his stepdaughter, was really his...well...he still couldn't get his mind around it.

"No, no, that is not true my dear, I had really no clue, believe me," he was stuttering, "I thought you forgot what you were claiming that . . . that . . ."

Linda sat up ready in bed, "See. See. Say it, Tom!" Tom frowned and his mouth twisted up, but no sound came.

"Claiming what?" Linda continued. "Claiming that I am Jessica, which is who I am?" Linda was speaking with force. "If you ask, I didn't forget. I can't forget. Can you forget who you are, Tom?"

"I had no idea." Tom said, looking into her eyes. It was as if he was seeing her for the first time. "I thought . . . I thought that Jessica was somehow using you as a medium to communicate with me and with Angela."

Linda shook her head. "Linda doesn't exist. I'm Jessica. All these years I've been trapped in a child's body that's masquerading as someone else. Do you see, Tom, how much I had to suffer?" Bitterness crept into her tone. "Living with my husband and my sister. Watching you living intimately together. Sleeping in one bedroom together like husband and wife. Kissing each other and making love in front of my eyes. And I . . . I have to conceal my feelings, hide my tears and continue my damned life in this weird situation. Why? Because I love you. I didn't stop loving you, Tom. I loved my sister, too. I don't want to hurt her. I don't want to hurt anybody. I've no idea how all this came about. I just know that it did, that's all. And we have to deal with it." She stopped and wiped away a tear.

Linda no longer looked to Tom like a typical American teenager in sweatshirt and blue jeans. It was as if she was metamorphosing in front of his eyes.

After a moment's pause, Linda said with urgency, "Did I express myself well? Do you know what I feel now?"

"Yes, I do," Tom said. While looking at Linda's face his thoughts were fixed on Jessica, his dead wife who was not dead at all.

"No, you don't," Linda said holding his hands, "Tom. I feel betrayed even though you both didn't do it on purpose. For God's sake. Call me at least by my real name. It comforts me. Is that too much to ask? It makes me feel I am what I am in reality."

"It's all right, Jessica," Tom said, feeling like he was actually talking to Jessica.

"Did you know what I do when I'm alone here?" Linda said, fighting back tears. "I open my door and shout as loud as I can, Oh, Mighty God give me my life back! Tom please help me, I want my life back!"

She turned her face away, crying silently. Tom sat on the edge of the bed, stunned. Linda was behaving exactly as Jessica used to when she was upset--the expressions she used were similar, and even her gestures and facial expressions conveyed the flavor of the late Jessica.

Linda was a genuine reproduction of Jessica. He extended his hand to her slowly and tried to pull her shoulder, saying: "Jessica, I am really very sorry to let you suffer. I didn't know. What could I do? I promise not to do it again."

Linda turned to Tom slowly, looking into his eyes. She seemed to be searching for something, some reassurance that he was in earnest. She held his arm and slowly approached near him. Then she smiled with tears still in her eyes. Tom got another flash of recognition. That was exactly what Jessica used to do--when he used to comfort her, an easy smile would suddenly appear on her face even when she was close to tears.

Suddenly, before Tom could say another word, she embraced him and kissed him many times, whispering, "Oh my love, you can't imagine how much I love you, and how much I longed to hold you in my arms like this."

Tom couldn't resist her sudden emotional outpouring but at the same time he was perplexed and his heart was divided. He closed his eyes and felt that it really was Jessica holding and kissing him. He wanted to comfort her while she poured out her feelings. But instead he found that he was the one who was being comforted, by the feeling of Jessica's presence. He felt that something he had lost for all these years was now in his hands again. Something real, made of flesh and blood. He felt sorry for all the girl's suffering and felt that he should have shown more courage in facing up to the situation and trying to understand it. He was stirred by her kisses and aroused by the way she was whispering in his ear--just like Jessica had done, all those years ago. He couldn't deny that he enjoyed the moments he was holding Linda in his arms, feeling Jessica herself kissing and talking to him. He now believed that she was Jessica herself. And yet, thrashing around in the back of his mind, was the terrifying thought that he was about to embark on an affair with what the rest of the world would regard as his fourteen-year-old stepdaughter. Tom could hardly begin to imagine the problems that might lie ahead.

Linda was laughing. "I'm so happy," she said, as Tom continued to hold her in his arms, dreaming of Jessica. "Can you imagine how long I've waited for this moment?" Linda said.

Tom remembered back to when Linda was four years old when he had found her at midnight in the basement, wearing Jessica's dress and gazing into the mirror. "I'll get you, Tom," she had said. And now she had.

After some time had elapsed, Tom said he had to go back downstairs to make sure that Angela was all right.

"Don't tell her what we did, O.K.?" Linda whispered.

Tom nodded.

That night, when Tom went to bed, he couldn't sleep. Neither could Angela. They both lay there, silent, he on his back and she on her side, each lost in their own thoughts about the situation.

It was Angela who broke the silence. "Can you tell me what are we going to do?" she asked in a low voice.

"I don't have a solution," Tom whispered.

"Can you stay at home tomorrow after Linda leaves for school?"

"Why?"

"I have something to show you."

"O.K. I'll stay."

Angela went to the bathroom to take a sleeping pill. Tom didn't take pills. He would sooner have a sleepless night. His thoughts roamed restlessly, back and forth, on Jessica and Linda, the past and the present.

= CHAPTER 5 =

The following morning, Linda came downstairs looking somewhat cheerful. She had done something different with her hair, which made it look more like Jessica's hair, even though Linda did not have Jessica's striking flame-red hair. Linda also wore Jessica's dress instead of her usual blue jeans. She was wearing make-up and looked much older than her fourteen years.

Angela concealed the alarm she felt as she noticed Linda's appearance.

"You look very nice today with your make up," she said, then looked at Tom, to encourage him to confirm her statement. Angela wanted things to appear normal while she figured out what, if anything, she could do about this extremely disturbing situation.

Tom took the hint and made a positive comment. Linda received both their remarks with a smile. She didn't seem to assume that Angela was making some kind of veiled criticism of her, which had often been the way over the past few months.

She looked at Tom and said, "Tom, I feel very happy today."

"I'm glad to hear that . . . Jessica," Tom replied, looking at her and smiling broadly.

"I want to eat with you today, Tom," Linda said. This was unusual because normally Linda did not eat breakfast.

Linda glanced at Angela but Angela made no reaction. Then Angela got up and went to the kitchen to fetch something. Linda looked across at Tom and gave him a winning smile.

"Thanks, Tom, for calling me in my real name in front of Angela," she said cheerfully. "She must acquaint herself with it."

While eating and talking with Tom, it seemed to him that she was Jessica in every word she said and every gesture she made. She didn't mention school or anything about her own life. Instead, just as Jessica used to do, she talked to him about his work, and then asked if he would be coming home early that night. She warned him not to come too late.

When Tom reminded her that it was time to go to school she said, laughing: "You want to get rid of me, Tom?"

When Linda was ready to go, she held Tom's head and gave him a long kiss.

"Wipe off the rouge before you go out," she whispered. "Have a good day, Tom. And remember, don't come home too late."

"O.K. Jessica. Take care."

It felt strange to Tom to call her Jessica after she had been Linda all those years, and yet he felt he was now calling her by her real name. His mind was still in turmoil over what this all meant and how it could possibly have happened, but he was resolving to tackle each situation as it came up and hope that everything would resolve itself.

Before she closed the front door after her, Linda called out loudly,"Bye Angela!"

Angela came out of the kitchen glowering. Her face was pale.

"What's wrong?" said Tom, hearing alarm bells going off in his head.

"There is nothing wrong with me, Dad," Angela said, mocking him. She handed him a paper napkin. "I saw how you two kissing, like lovers. Wipe off your lips."

"Ah, come on, Angela." Tom knew he had to calm her down, "She's only a child. She needs help psychological support."

"So you helped her with your kissing treatment?" Angela shouted."You and your psychological support. Come upstairs, I'll show you something."

She hurried upstairs. Tom followed her. She opened Linda's door and went directly to the bed, where she felt around under the mattress and pillows. But she couldn't find the diary. The book had disappeared. She looked under the bed, and in the drawers. There was no diary. Angela sat on the edge of the bed holding her head in her hands. She began to sob.

"What were you searching for?" Tom asked.

"Her diary."

"A diary?"

Tom had no idea that Linda kept a diary, although he remembered that Jessica did. She would never let an event go by without writing something about it. He decided he would search the house for Linda's diary, but he preferred not to tell Angela.

"All the photos have disappeared," Angela said.

"What photos?"

"Jessica's photos, of course."

"Angela, I don't know why you're looking for her diary. What are you trying to prove?"

"To show you the real Linda."

"Angela, I know who Linda is." Tom took her hands and looked into her eyes, "As you yourself said, Linda is not your daughter. She is Jessica. We should both admit it. You must accept it as I now have. I don't know what to do about it. What's happened is beyond my knowledge. I don't understand it at all. But we have to learn to live with it."

"Tom, many years ago I told you to make sure she got treatment." Angela was ready to blame him. "But you never listened to me."

"You know as well as I do what the psychiatrist said. What could she do about it? Nothing. She said Jessica . . . Linda, was fine."

"I'm sure there must be some kind of treatment," Angela insisted. "There must be some kind of help. Otherwise this is just too weird. I can't go on living in this situation."

"Shall we start again, Angela?" Tom said firmly, "What can we say to convince her that we have to take her to a doctor? To treat her for what disease? Madness or what?"

"We can tell we're taking her for a check up, that's all," Angela said.

"But she's not sick," Tom shook his head. "She knows she doesn't need to see a doctor. She is very healthy and intelligent. You know she doesn't even need to study and in spite of that she still gets high grades. You know what Linda said to me? She said she had already read these boring lessons before."

"I'll go to Dr. Johnson to discuss the problem with him," Angela said. "Maybe he has a better idea."

Tom was not convinced. But he didn't want to argue with Angela. He could tell that she was desperate for a way of dealing with the situation. So was he. But he was trying not to think about it.

* * *

"My dear Angela, this subject is not my field. I am a general practitioner," Dr. Peter Johnson said. "Given the symptoms that you have described, this case is for a psychiatrist with experience in psychoanalysis and hypnotism. I would suggest that you take Linda to Dr. White. He practices hypnotism. He is well known in this field with a lot of experience."

Angela and Tom were both sitting uncomfortably in one of the treatment rooms at the offices of their family doctor. Tom had allowed Angela to explain the reason for their visit. He watched Dr. Johnson carefully for his reaction. As Tom listened to Angela explain, it did seem a fantastic story. Would the doctor think they were crazy?

Dr. Johnson, who was a balding man in late middle age, with a quiet manner, did not betray much reaction. If he thought they were crazy, he wasn't saying.

"Dr. Johnson," Tom began. "How can we take Linda to Dr. White without any obvious reason? I mean a reason to convince her to accept--"

"Well the reason is obvious, isn't it? She appears to believe that she is your former wife--"

"Come on, Dr. Johnson," Tom replied, letting his annoyance show. "It's more than that. Linda knows she is Jessica. She doesn't just believe it. And I believe her too. She is my wife Jessica. Even if it sounds crazy, that's the reality. If she needs treatment, I need it too."

"All right, all right," said Dr. Johnson, in the calming voice that he must have used on thousands of upset patients. "I'll make it easy for you. Just bring Linda to me, or just send her on her own. I'll convince her that it would be in her best interests to make an appointment with Dr. White."

"But what will we tell her to get her to come to you? I'm afraid she will refuse," Angela said.

"That is your problem, I think," Dr Johnson replied, having obviously decided that there were limits to how helpful he was prepared to be.

Tom left the clinic very upset. Angela didn't want to talk about it at all.

* * *

That night Angela knocked on Linda's door to say goodnight. Her mind was in turmoil. It was all so eerie, so strange, like something out of a movie. Her sister had gone. She had died. People don't come back from the dead and take over other bodies. It just doesn't happen. Angela had done her grieving many years ago and Jessica was now a sweet memory. But all this business with Linda was stirring everything up again. What should she do? Should she try to talk to Linda as Jessica, or should she just try to reconnect with Linda as her daughter? There were still times when Linda was just like any other fourteen-year-old, with the same insecurities about her appearance and avid interest in whatever rock band was currently top of the charts.

Angela tried to imagine calling her daughter Jessica, but the name stuck in her throat. She knew she couldn't do it. But what else could she do? She floundered around in a state of indecision, and it was in this state of mind that she was knocking on Linda's door. She had no plan at all for what she was going to say.

She heard Linda stop what she was doing and come to the door quickly. But there was no mistaking the look of disappointment on her face when she saw who her visitor was. It didn't take Angela long to conclude that Linda had thought it would be Tom.

"Ah! It's you," Linda said coldly and returned to her bed. She showed no desire to talk.

"I came to wish you goodnight," Angela said as she entered. "I saw the light was on. Do you have much to read?"

Linda lay down on her bed. Angela sat on the chair at the foot of the bed and tried to initiate a conversation. But Linda would barely respond.

"I'm not in the mood to talk," Linda said. She just stared up at the ceiling.

Angela quickly decided that she would not get anywhere with Linda whatever she said, so she stood up to leave. "It seems you want to sleep."

"No. I can't sleep," Linda said.

"Why can't you sleep?" Angela asked.

"Do you have nightmares or something?"

"Why do you ask?"

"Just wondering. You shouldn't have trouble sleeping at your age. I don't sleep well either. Sometimes I take sleeping pills."

"Do they work?"

"Yes. Almost always."

Suddenly Linda seemed interested.

"What are you thinking, Linda?" Angela asked.

Linda started to pout. Angela guessed why--it must be because she had called her Linda. Angela felt she made a mistake, but then felt annoyed with herself for thinking that. After all, what else could she call her daughter, whom she had christened Linda? Confused, she turned to walk out of the room. "Sleep well!" she said.

"Can you give me a tablet of yours?" Linda asked.

Angela stopped and turned back. "Do you really think you need a tablet to sleep?"

"Yes, why not? I can't sleep well. You use them."

"But I can't give you one of mine," Angela said.

"Why not?"

"Well, these were prescribed for me. You're still young. I'm afraid to give you a tablet that could hurt you."

"How could it hurt me if it doesn't hurt you?" Then her face fell. "I don't want it anyway," she said.

Angela suddenly had an idea. This might be the opportunity they had needed.

"I think it's safer to ask Dr. Johnson about it," Angela said. "He'll know whether it's the right thing to give you some medication to help you sleep. Something that suits your age and condition."

"All right, I'll go to see him tomorrow," Linda said, in an indifferent tone of voice.

* * *

An hour or so later, Angela had gone to bed, but Tom was still up, working in his study. He was putting the finishing touches to a presentation that he was to make to an important client, and he didn't notice the quiet footsteps approaching the study door.

Linda stood in the doorway. She had put on a thin nightgown, brushed her hair, and sneaked out from her bedroom. She stood a while, barefoot, looking at Tom, as he worked steadily at his computer.

Suddenly he sensed something and looked up and around. When he saw Linda he stopped working. Linda entered the room and closed the door behind her. She took a few steps forward.   "Don't stop, Tom," she whispered, "I like watching you working as before. You look important."

"I can't work when somebody's watching me," Tom said, smiling.

"I know that, Tom. I don't want to keep you from your work. I just came down to drink something and to say goodnight."

She walked around the table and came close to him. "Don't work too much, Tom," she said, looking into his eyes.

"Why not?"

"I want you to stay young until I am eighteen," Linda said, caressing his cheek.

"Eighteen?" Tom asked. He suddenly felt alarmed.

Linda didn't say any more. She came closer, and put her arm across his shoulders. Then she hopped onto his lap and started kissing him.

Tom was taken by surprise, and once more he got an eerie feeling. He couldn't help but recall how Jessica used to come down to him every night before she went to bed. She would sit in his lap just the way Linda was doing, and kiss him goodnight--just the way Linda was doing now. He allowed her to kiss him but he was also filled with a strange unease. He also found himself waiting to see if afterwards Linda tried to stand and pull him up from his chair.

"I don't want to interrupt you. You don't belong totally to me," Linda whispered, "We have to share you, Angela and me, for the time being, of course." She wriggled off his lap and then stood up and leaned her head on his shoulder, biting his ear tenderly--just as Jessica used to do. Then finally she took him by both hands and pulled him up from the chair. It was then that Tom noticed that Linda was wearing the same perfume that Jessica had done. That pleasant, evocative fragrance transported him back in time. He could no longer resist. For a moment, it seemed to him as if he were living in a trance. Linda was pulling him into the past where he was with Jessica again. He forgot himself and allowed the rapture to sweep over him. He took Linda in his arms and closed his eyes, rocked her gently and kissed her. He was back in his sweet memories of the past with Jessica. She, his darling Jessica, whom he had loved so well, and missed so badly--and missed her still, even after all these fourteen years. He didn't allow himself to think of what the future might hold. This moment, now, was enough.

* * *

In the morning, Linda came down for breakfast wearing Jessica's dress. It was the same dress which she put on when she was four years old. Even now, it was still a bit big for her.

"Jessica, you can't wear that dress as is," Tom said softly. "It needs some changes."

"Do you think so?" Linda said in a friendly tone. Tom was relieved that she hadn't taken his comment as a criticism.

"Well, I agree," said Linda. "It needs to be taken in a little. I can do it later. I'll wear something else today."

She went back upstairs to change. Tom went to help Angela, who was in the kitchen preparing breakfast. Angela told him about her conversation with Linda the previous night.

"I suggested that she could go to Dr. Johnson," Angela whispered, "Call him now and remind him of our discussion."

Linda came down wearing the same dress she had worn the day before. She stood in front of Tom.

"Is this OK?" she said.

"Yes, Jessica, it's very nice," Tom replied.

"Do you really mean it, Tom?"

"Yes, dear Jessica."

Linda smiled when she heard herself addressed as Jessica. And when she heard "dear Jessica" she almost purred with pleasure.

Angela heard what had been said and felt angry and confused again. "Can you help me with the breakfast, please, Linda?" she called out from the kitchen.

Linda winked at Tom, smiling. Tom noticed that she didn't react badly to Angela calling her "Linda," as had happened before. He guessed that she was satisfied because he had shown that he accepted her as Jessica.

* * *

After Linda set off for school, Tom called Dr. Johnson. He couldn't reach him directly, and left a message with the receptionist. A few minutes later Dr. Johnson was on the phone.

"Yes, Tom, what's new?" Dr. Johnson asked.

"Do you remember our discussion about sending Linda to you?"

"Yes, yes, what about it?"

"Well, she may be coming in for an appointment."

"Ah. You managed to persuade her then--"

"No, doctor, I didn't," Tom interrupted. "It came up in another context. She says she's had difficulty sleeping, so she told Angela she wanted to get some sleeping pills from you."

"Sleeping pills at her age? I'll talk to her and find out what's going on."

"Please, doctor, try to win her confidence," Tom said.

"I'll do my best."

"I think it might be better not to mention, at least on her first visit to you, anything about what we discussed about the matter of Jessica, please. I think she'd just clam up and then we'd never get to the bottom of it."

"Well, as I told you, this is really a matter for Dr. White--"

"Yes, but just this time, please just help her with the pills, if that's what she needs, that's all,"

"All right Tom, I'll assess her general physical health and if she needs some temporary medication, I'll prescribe it."

Tom felt relieved. He wanted to keep the lid on this can of worms for a while longer, if he could. Maybe he could figure out on his own how to handle it if he did a little bit of reading and research. On reflection, he thought that was better than handing Jessica . . . Linda, over to the shrinks. He resolved to find time later that day to visit the library or bookstore.

= CHAPTER 6 =

Instead of going to school, Linda took the fifteen-minute walk to Dr. Johnson's clinic. It was a cool, fresh fall morning. Fallen leaves were beginning to gather on sidewalks and lawns.

Linda took the opportunity to think hard about her life. Her mind went back to that fateful evening over fourteen years ago, when she, as Jessica, had gone for that ill-advised drive in the storm. The memory of it was vivid, and had been since Linda was little, although she could not recall all the details. It was more the feeling of it all that haunted her. She could see in her mind's eye the dark and rainy night. She knew she was driving too fast but she wanted to get home before the storm got any worse. She couldn't see what was in front of her, even though the windshield wipers were dancing at maximum speed across the glass.

She remembered a moment of horror as something huge suddenly was bearing down on her from nowhere . . . She remembered calling out, "Tom! Tom!" as the truck smashed into the front of her car. Then everything was blank and dark and she was swimming in nothingness. Then slowly she came back to consciousness and found herself in another dark place, warm and confined, but before she had a chance to explore it she found herself being plucked into the dazzling light...but now everything had changed from when she was Jessica Wells. Everything was confused and foggy, and she could not express the thoughts and feelings that were racing through her mind and heart. All she could do was cry and cry...she felt weak and helpless, and then she was wrapped up in a cloth and presented to her sister, Angela.

It had been a long, long fourteen years. She had learned to fake another identity, that of Linda, Angela's daughter, because she had quickly figured out what was expected of her. Indeed, sometimes it even seemed to her that there were two beings, two souls, inside that one tiny body. One she knew intimately, and that was herself, Jessica; the other was the child Linda, to whom the world was totally new, and who had to learn how to do things with her growing body and mind. Jessica/Linda grew up with a kind of dual awareness. She was both Jessica and Linda. But as she reached puberty one desire grew in her heart and one desire only. She was sick of masquerading as a child, as the daughter of her sister, and the stepchild of Tom, *her own beloved husband*! It had to stop. She wanted Tom. She wanted him as she had had him in the past, as lover and husband. She knew him intimately. She had won him once and she would do so again. She knew this would devastate Angela. But she found that her heart was hardening towards her sister, who had taken her husband from her. She has always competed with me, going right back to the time we were in high school together, so why shouldn't I fight back now? Linda thought to herself. Why should I bother with what Angela might think? I have to do what I have to do, and that's all there is to it. A plan formed in her mind.

She reached the clinic, and had to wait for a while before Dr. Johnson could squeeze her into his schedule.

"Good morning Dr. Johnson," Linda said. She was a bit nervous.

"Hey Linda," Dr. Johnson said, "How are you today?"

"Well, I came after I discussed something with Angela ... I mean my mm...moth...mother," Linda stammered. It was the hardest thing in the world for Linda to refer to Angela as her mother, even though she realized people expected it.

"I can't sleep well. Angela told me to come to you. I asked her to give me one of her pills, but she wouldn't."

Dr. Johnson nodded and began to ask her a series of questions about her health. Linda told him that she couldn't sleep as well as she used to.

"I mean, I lie in bed for hours before I fall asleep."

"Does this happen every night, or just sometimes?" Dr. Johnson asked.

"It seems to be every night now."

"Do you dream sweet dreams?" Dr. Johnson asked, with a smile and twinkle in his eye.

"Sometimes, really sweet dreams, but mostly nightmares."

Linda did not mention what the sweet dreams consisted of, or the nightmares. Fortunately, Dr. Johnson did not ask. But Linda knew that the dreams were of Tom--Tom and her, together, making love, just as they had done before. And the nightmares were of losing him, of growing older and seeing Tom still with Angela, her kid sister--the kid sister winning the most important competition they had ever had. She couldn't allow that to happen. And that was what occupied her in the hours before she fell asleep. How to make it happen. How to get her Tom back.

"All right, Linda," Dr. Johnson said eventually. "I'll give you some mild pills that will help you sleep."

"Thank you, doctor." Linda was happy to hear that.

"It's important that you don't take more than the allowed dosage," Dr. Johnson warned. "You may take only half a tablet per day. We'll see how you do with that."

"How do they taste, doctor?" Linda asked concerned.

Dr. Johnson laughed. "They taste a bit bitter. But that's not important because you are going to swallow them with some water or juice."

"Dr. Johnson, I don't want them if they're bitter. Do you have some that don't taste bitter, I mean tasteless? Please!"

"Alright, I'll give you another sort that's not bitter,"

"Thanks. But if half a tablet doesn't help, what shall I do? Shall I take another half or one tablet?"

"No, Linda, never!" Dr. Johnson raised his voice. "I told you. Don't take more than one-half of a tablet, whatever the circumstances. That's the maximum dose for you. Not more than that. Got it?"

"I understand. But what shall I do then, if I still can't sleep?"

"Come back to see me and I'll help you! O.K.?"

Linda left the doctor's office, feeling lighter and happier. She had taken steps to improve her situation, and that always felt good.

* * *

"What did the doctor say?" Angela asked later in the day when Linda returned from school.

"Who?" Linda said, pretending that the matter was not so important.

"Dr. Johnson of course."

"Who told you I went?"

"Nobody. Well, you did actually. Remember, you said you would see him today?

"Well if you're interested," Linda said indifferently, "nothing happened really."

"Did he prescribe something?"

"Yeah!" Linda replied, trying to appear unconcerned, as if it was no big deal. "He gave me a medical sample from his drawer. That's all." After a moment, Linda continued, "He gave me the sample and said it would help me to sleep. "

"Nothing else?" Angela asked again.

"That's it!" Linda said as she went upstairs, "He said that would help me. If it doesn't I have to go back to him."

Linda didn't want to go into details. In fact, she no longer wished to speak to Angela at all, but she didn't want to arouse any suspicions. At the moment, she knew that no one had any idea of what was brewing in her head. What she was planning. The recent breakthroughs she had made with Tom, his responsive attitude and his open heart, have given her fresh impetus to free herself from her weird life.

First of all, she thought, she must make sure that she had enough time with Tom undisturbed. That meant that Angela must somehow be removed from the scene. It might be possible to meet Tom outside, but that would be difficult to arrange. Inside wouldn't be any easier thought. It seemed as if Angela was always there. Linda couldn't talk with Tom without Angela being present as well. Angela also seemed to have a knack for hearing everything that went on in the house--as long as she was awake, that is.

Linda knew that Angela slept soundly whenever she took a sleeping pill, but she also knew that Angela didn't want to become dependent on the pills, so she didn't take them every night. The problem was that Linda had no way of knowing which nights Angela took the medication. It wasn't possible for her to watch Angela all the time to see if she took her pills or not. If she only took the pill regularly every night--whether knowingly or not-- it would be easier to control the situation. Then, Linda thought, she would be able to have a good time with Tom every night, when it got late, without Angela's interference. She would have long hours of serenity and pleasure with Tom, just as she had had before, without interruption. She imagined such evenings, talking to Tom, kissing him and making love to him, just like before she had "died." Linda didn't really think of that episode as a death. It was just transformation that was all.

She used to live in a certain body; now she lived in another one that was all. Some people referred to her as Linda, but she was still Jessica. She would always be Jessica. It didn't seem strange to her that this had happened. It seemed the most natural thing in the world. It was because she and Tom were meant to be together through all eternity, and nothing could prevent that.

* * *

After dinner, Linda was watching the TV. She heard Tom calling to Angela from his study, asking her to make him a cup of coffee. Linda got up and went to the kitchen.

"I can help," Linda said to Angela. "I'll make Tom's coffee."

"Oh! Thank you," Angela said. Surprised by Linda's initiative. "Do you know how he likes it?"

"Yes, I know," Linda said, looking at Angela and smiling with confidence. "Strong with a little creamer."

"That's right," Angela said, still surprised. "Only one teaspoonful creamer. I wonder how much you know that I don't know about."

Linda ignored the implication of this. "Go and sit, and I'll take care of it," she said, still smiling. "Do you want a cup too?"

"You want to make coffee for me also?"

"Yes, I'd love to!" Linda said.

"I don't think I want to drink coffee now," Angela said. "It keeps me awake."

"I see," Linda said. "How about a tea or cocoa?"

"A cup of tea is all right, thank you Linda! Oh! I'm sorry, I meant Jessica."

Linda couldn't tell whether Angela meant this sarcastically, and she didn't react to it. She no longer cared much about what Angela thought anyway.

She prepared the coffee and took it to Tom in the study, leaving the tea to brew. Angela was in the sitting room watching TV.

"Tom darling, here's your coffee," Linda said in her sweetest voice.

"Oh, thanks Jessica! It was very nice of you."

"Did I surprise you," Linda asked, laughing.

"Did you surprise me?" Tom repeated, "Yes, you did, it was a nice surprise, dear."

She leaned forward, putting her elbows on the computer and holding her head with both hands. Tom looked at her. She smiled at him.

"Taste your coffee," she said. "I made it just for you."

"Oh, you did!" Tom said, sipping, "This is another surprise."

"Don't say it just to encourage me," Linda said, laughing.

"Jessica dear, I meant it, really."

Linda smiled and went back to check on the tea.

"Are you in the kitchen, Linda?" Angela called out. When she didn't hear an answer she went to the kitchen.

"Why didn't you answer me?" Angela asked.

"What did you want?" Linda asked.

This time she was offended by what she thought was Angela's deliberate use of her false name in order to get at her.

"Why are you angry? What did I do now?" Angela asked, genuinely surprised.

"Because you never quit calling me Linda," Linda said, raising her voice. "I am not Linda. I'm Jessica. I've told you so many times. Is that clear?"

"Yes dear, I know. I'm sorry. But I can't change in one day." Angela said, thinking that the best thing to do was pacify this annoying daughter of hers and keep her real thoughts to herself.

"Tom could," Linda said.

"Well, I'm not Tom. I need time to adapt. Is it OK with you?"

"Yeah! What did you want?"

"I? No. Nothing," Angela said and left the kitchen.

"I'm making tea for you" Linda called out.

"I don't want it," Angela said.

Linda poured a cup of tea into a mug and took it to the sitting room.

"Here's your tea," Linda said, softly. "Please tell me if it's all right or not."

"I don't want it," Angela said, still irritated, "You can drink it yourself."

"Come on, Angela," Linda said. This wasn't what she had been planning on. She needed to show Angela that she genuinely wanted to be helpful in the kitchen.

"I'm sorry," Linda said. "I couldn't help it."

Angela was surprised at the sudden change in Linda's attitude and thought she ought to reward her. She smiled at Linda and took the cup from her.

"Now I want to make a cup of cocoa for me," Linda went back to the kitchen, prepared some cocoa and took it upstairs.

Before going to her bedroom she went to Angela's bedroom and rummaged around until she found Angela's sleeping tablets. When she found the packet she removed one tablet and placed it in her pocket. Once inside her bedroom, she closed the door, took out the pill and tasted it. It was bitter. Then she took out one of her own tablets and tasted it. It was not as bitter; in fact it was almost tasteless, just as Dr. Johnson had said it would be. She was satisfied with her little experiment. Nobody would be aware of the presence of the tablet if she put it in coffee or tea.

She took half a tablet and put it in the cocoa and stirred it. She tasted the mixture carefully, and was convinced that nobody would notice anything strange about the taste. She took the other half of the tablet, threw it in the cup and stirred again. She tasted the cocoa again. The taste didn't change.

She lifted the cup and sipped a little more, enjoying the result.

She didn't really have insomnia, of course. Bad dreams, yes, she had those. But they were not new and she knew how to deal with them. Her plan wasn't to treat herself; it never had been. She was going to "treat" Angela, making sure that Angela took a sleeping tablet daily. This would leave Linda free to spend longer times with Tom every night. But she had to win Angela's confidence by showing her that she, Linda, liked doing things in the kitchen, such as helping in the preparation of coffee and tea. She had to pretend to show satisfaction when Angela praised her. It was important that Angela believe that Linda really wanted to work in the kitchen in order to learn something. Fortunately, Linda thought to herself as she sipped more cocoa, she was good at acting. She always had been. And when she had been known as Jessica, she had a reputation for being strong-willed and getting what she wanted. In that respect, nothing had changed at all.

She drank half of the cocoa and went downstairs to kiss Tom goodnight. Tom was sitting with Angela watching TV.

"What do you think Tom?" Linda asked, "Can I make coffee? This time Angela helped me."

"I didn't help her at all," Angela said to Tom. "She did it alone."

"It was really good coffee," Tom said. "If I'm ever not satisfied with your coffee, I'll tell you, but don't be angry then. Promise?"

"I'll never be angry with you!"

"She only gets angry at me," Angela interjected with a smile.

"Jessica can't be angry at her beloved sister. Goodnight!" Linda smiled at Angela and then promptly turned around and went back upstairs before Angela could react.

* * *

Next morning, Linda didn't come down for breakfast at the usual time. Angela called up to her. When she didn't hear an answer, she went upstairs. She opened Linda's door and found her still in bed asleep.

"Linda . . . I mean Jessica, wake up!" Angela said, "You'll miss the first hour of school."

Linda woke up immediately and was not very pleased to find her mother/sister bending over her, a look of concern on her face. Linda felt tired. She sat up in bed rubbing her eyes.

"What's the time now, Angela?"

"Eight o'clock. What happened to you?" Angela asked, "Did you take one of your pills yesterday?"

Linda recalled the events of the previous evening. She remembered that the effect of the pill was not immediate. It had taken an hour or so before she relaxed and fell asleep.

"No. No I didn't. I couldn't sleep. I slept late."

"Why didn't you try the pills?"

"I don't know why. OK?"

Linda got out of bed, grabbed her towel and went to take a shower. By the time she came downstairs, Tom had already gone. She was disappointed.

"When did Tom leave?" she asked.

"He left about ten minutes ago. He has a client to see. Why?"

"Why didn't he wait for me before he left?"

Angela just shrugged.

Linda reached for her bag in a hurry and slammed the door behind her saying, "Bye, Angela." She couldn't get out of the door fast enough. Then she realized that if she was going to get along with Angela, she was going to have to try a lot harder.

$=$ CHAPTER 7 $=$

"Do you think this lecture would be of any benefit for us?" Angela asked. She was looking at a notice in the newspaper that Tom had shown her.

"Maybe, maybe not," Tom replied. "But I think it's worth a try. We don't hear a lecture of this kind every day. I mean about reincarnation. Can't we go together?"

"Tom, I don't know. I don't have any reason to go and hear some meaningless lecture. It's not going to help."

"Angela, please, I want you to come with me just this one time. It won't take more than an hour or so. Remember what I was saying about the book I was reading?"

Tom had found time to get to the bookstore. He had found several interesting books about parapsychology, and a short, remarkable book about reincarnation. He had sat up virtually all night reading the reincarnation book, much to Angela's annoyance. Tom had never read anything like it. It turned out that there were quite a number of recorded cases, many of them in India, but in other parts of the world too, about people recalling a past life, and knowing details about it that they could not have found out from any known source. Sometimes children would know exact geographical locations of where they had formerly lived, and know the names of members of their former family. One woman in Europe had recurring dreams of a certain village in Ireland, and memories of a woman dying in childbirth. Numerous details later confirmed, when she visited

Ireland that she herself was the woman who had died, some forty years earlier. Members of her former family were so convinced of her story that the men who were the sons of the woman who had died (who were now about the same age as the woman herself) began calling her mother.

It was an eye opener for Tom. But he couldn't find any examples of spouses mysteriously taking on new incarnations within the immediate family that they had just left. They were always reincarnated some distance away, without any obvious link to their new families. Until now, thought Tom. He wondered whether Jessica was indeed a completely unique phenomenon. What had caused her to return? Was it because she loved him so much? But how could he return her love in the way she wanted, when she was still only a child, and he already had a wife, who happened to be his dead wife's sister?

Tom's curiosity had been awakened, as well as his need to solve the problem, and that was why he was proposing to attend the lecture, which was by a world expert on parapsychology.

After a few more minutes of wrangling about it, Angela said, "O.K. if you insist. When is it?"

"Tomorrow at seven P.M."

"What's going on with you, Tom? I noticed you reading all those strange books."

"Do you mean spiritual books? You know, you can learn a lot--"

"You mean I'll find it interesting," Angela said. "But I don't think anybody will understand all these so-called metaphysical phenomena, ever. We're flesh and blood not spirits."

"Well, I understand what you mean. But it's not about calling forth spirits or discussing Halloween ghosts."

"Anyway, who's the lecturer?"

"He's a psychiatrist from the University of Philadelphia. I'd like to try to get to talk to him after the lecture."

"You mean, ask him ?"

"Yes. Why not? This is what I intend to do."

"Tom, be careful. I don't think this matter should be discussed so openly."

"Why not? I don't mean during the lecture, but just quietly with him in person after the lecture."

"I don't agree with you, Tom. We just have to live with what we've got. We're never going to understand it."

Angela got up from the couch and went to the kitchen to make coffee. Just at that moment, Linda, who had doing some homework in her room, decided to come down and join them. She sat on the couch next to Tom.

"Honey, your mother . . . I mean Angela . . was sitting here," Tom said.

"She can sit anywhere else," Linda said, without a trace of concern. "My place is near you, Tom. Remember?" Linda called out to Angela in the kitchen,

"Angela! What are you doing?"

"Yes dear," Angela said.

"But I told you I wanted to make the coffee for you," Linda said, sounding disappointed.

"I thought you wanted to make coffee only for Tom."

"I meant for both of you and for me too."

"All right, come and take over."

Linda jumped up and then leaned over to kiss Tom. When she got to the kitchen she said, "Angela, why didn't you call me down to help?"

"I thought you were busy in your studies," said Angela, not wishing to make an issue of it.

"You go and sit down," Linda said, "I'll bring the drinks in when they're ready."

"The coffee is for Tom, and--"

"And the tea for you. I know," Linda said.

"Please make it the same as yesterday."

After a few minutes Linda emerged into the sitting room carrying three cups: coffee, tea and cocoa. They all sat and drank silently, watching the TV, Tom in the middle, Angela and Linda on either side.

After a while Angela said, "By the way, Linda--sorry, I meant Jessica--tomorrow evening Tom and I are going out."

"Where are you going?" Linda asked curiously, looking across at Tom.

"We're going to a lecture," Angela said.

"When?" Linda asked.

"Seven P.M. It may take one or two hours. Don't you think so, Tom?"

"It could be. But we won't be late," Tom said.

"What kind of lecture is it?" Linda asked Tom," Is it something boring about taxes or business stuff?"

"I think it would be boring for you, anyway," Angela said, looking to Tom to get his support.

"In that case I prefer to stay at home," Linda said, looking to Tom. "Tom, can you stay with me and let Angela go?"

"No, Angela promised to go with me," Tom said.

"All right. If you go," Linda said, irritated, "I'll invite my friend to come over."

"Who is she?" Tom asked, interested.

"No, not she. It's he. Peter," Linda said, laughing.

"Who is Peter then?" Tom asked. He had never heard Linda speak of a Peter.

"One of my friends," Linda said smiling, trying to tease him.

"I must know who he is," Tom said with hardness in his voice.

"The one who accompanies me every day from school," Linda replied, delighted to see Tom's concern.

"Did you invite him here before?" Tom said; ready to interrogate her about this unexpected friend. "Was he here with you before?"

"I don't think so." Linda continued her teasing.

"You don't think so," Tom said irritated, "or you don't remember?"

"I said I don't think so." Linda was enjoying what she felt was Tom's concern. "I don't remember."

"How can you say you don't remember?" Tom was raising his voice. "Either he was here with you or he wasn't."

"No. He wasn't here," Linda said.

"Were you with him in his home then?" Tom asked, and then added before she could answer, "Or any other place?"

"Why are you asking me so many questions?" Linda snapped back. "What's going on? If you don't want me to bring him here, it's O.K. with me. But if you go out without me, I'll invite him."

"No, you won't," Tom shouted.

"Yes, I will."

As she said that, Linda jumped up and ran upstairs to her room, slamming the door behind her.

Angela turned towards Tom on the couch. "Why did you say all that?" she asked. She had kept quiet during the argument, deciding that it was better to just sip her tea and wait for the quarrel to pass.

"I don't know who this Peter is," replied Tom, still irritated. "Is he a good or a bad boy? She wanted to invite him in our absence. And you ask me why I wanted to know who he is?"

"Are you jealous?"

"Don't be ridiculous."

"But don't you want her to meet some boys and forget about her past? Don't you think that would be healthy for her? She needs to start forging a life for herself, and then maybe things will work out all right."

"Yes, yes of course," Tom replied, "but not at such a young age and in such circumstances. She's still young, she's immature and she's impulsive. She may make bad judgments, do something wrong."

"I don't think so," Angela said.

"What do you mean, I don't think so?"

"Well, she's mature enough to know what she's doing."

"I don't agree with you," Tom said, although in his heart he knew that Angela was right. He also wondered whether Angela was right about his being jealous of Linda attracting more male attention. He felt confused.

The conversation had petered out, and they spent another half an hour watching television. Angela felt sleepy.

"I think I have to go up. I feel tired," she said, "Are you coming?"

"No. I have work to do."

"O.K. then," Angela said, "Good night. When you come up I might already be asleep."

"Good night--sleep well."

Linda waited half an hour after Angela went to bed. Then she left her room and stood near Angela's door, listening. When she didn't hear any noise she opened the door slowly and listened again. Angela was faintly snoring.

"O.K. Angela. Sweet dreams?" she thought to herself.

= CHAPTER 8 =

Linda was pleased with herself. Her plan was working, and it had been very easy to put into effect. Now she would had enough time with Tom. She wondered why she hadn't thought of the sleeping pills before.

She returned to her room, brushed her hair, brushed her teeth and put on some light make up. Then she took her perfume spray and sprayed it on every part of her body. She looked in the mirror and was satisfied. She was ready to meet Tom, and she knew what she wanted.

When she opened the door to go downstairs, she was startled to find Tom standing at her door, arm raised, ready to knock. "Oh," she exclaimed, a bit flustered. Then she recovered. "Did you finish your work?" she said, taking Tom by the arm and pulling him inside the room. "I was coming down to say good night."

"No, Jessica, I didn't finish my work."

"Why not?" Linda said closing the door. Taking Tom's hand she led him to her bed, in preference to the one easy chair she had in her room.

"I couldn't concentrate on work."

"Why not?"

"Because of you, Jessica."

"Because of me? Why? What did I do?"

Linda sat on the bed and tugged at his arm so that he would sit beside her.

"Why did you say that you wanted to invite your boyfriend?"

"Why not, Tom? Do you forbid me?"

"But you with him alone?"

"What would happen?"

"Who knows what?"

"You mean, we might make love?"

"Yes. He may be a psycho or something…"

"Are you thinking of my safety?"

"Yes, of course I--"

"Or you are jealous of him?"

"Jessica, what is wrong with you?"

"There's nothing wrong with me. I think you're jealous, I like it. It makes me feel that you care for me," Linda said, pulling him closer to her. He did not resist.

"Don't worry Tom, I know he's peaceful. He may have had such an experience, but I think he hasn't yet."

"What do you mean? Experience of what?"

Tom turned towards her so that they were face to face. With his hands on both her shoulders, he gazed into her eyes to see whether she was serious or joking.

Linda felt she was in control of the situation, and relished her position. "Well, I meant Peter seems to me not experienced in sex, you know." She laughed. "So I thought I may give him a lesson in how to make love for dummies!"

"Oh no you won't, Jessica," Tom shot back, his brow furrowing. He felt a sudden surge of anger and hurt. He couldn't bear the thought of some young kid touching her, kissing her, making love to her. That was what he . . .

He sat with his head in his hands.

Linda said firmly, "Tom, are you jealous now? Now you know what I've felt all my life. I've had to watch my husband transferring his affections to my sister, while I got treated like his child."

"I am sorry, really sorry, I..." said Tom.

"Don't worry, Tom. Peter is not my boyfriend. I have no boyfriend... OK? I said that just to see how much you care for me."

"Of course I do care for you, Jessica."

"I got angry because Angela wanted to go out with you to have a good time. But I wanted to be alone with you."

"It wasn't to have fun. It was a lecture. A boring one. We told you."

"Tom, I missed you my whole life," Linda said, playing with his hair. "I wanted you to stay with me and let Angela go alone."

"No Jessica, I wanted to go to the lecture not she. I tried to convince her to go with me. She then agreed she would accompany me and come to the lecture. It won't take more than an hour or so. That's all. It's not such a big deal."

Linda sighed. "So what's it about, this lecture?" Linda asked, bringing her face closer to his, still playing with his hair.

"What?" Tom said. Her playful fingers were arousing his feelings, and he could smell her delectable perfume. That perfume made his mind race, and he wasn't concentrating on the conversation.

"The lecture," Linda repeated. "What's it about?"

"Oh, the lecture. It's about reincarnation."

"Reincarnation?" Linda took her hands from his face and looked serious. "You mean like me? Like my case? This lecture sounds like it's more for me than for either you or Angela."

"Yes, like your case."

"So I am one of those cases he is going to lecture about and analyze."

"Not you personally. No one knows about you. But yes, he's going to talk about similar cases, I think. But what he's going to say about them, I don't know."

"You know, Tom, I think you and Angela still don't really believe I'm Jessica," Linda said with bitterness. "But I say to you, nobody in the whole world can explain what I feel. Being one person in two bodies, or one soul in two lives, in two worlds. You've no idea what it's been like. What it's still like."

"Jessica, I can imagine--"

"Nonsense. Nobody could possibly understand how much I've suffered. I can remember just about everything of my previous life. It hasn't faded as I've grown up as Linda. It's got clearer. Can you imagine what that's like—it's like I'm split between two lives, two identities. But I know that Linda doesn't really exist as an independent person. She's all me, Jessica, *your* Jessica, but with a different appearance, that's all, and with some new experiences as this..." She started to cry and reached for a tissue. "Tom, can you imagine--when I was a child I knew I wasn't a child. I didn't feel like a child. Inside, I always felt like a mature adult. But I couldn't express it. And realized that in a sense I was a child--I had a child's body and I had to learn to do everything, just like a child does. You could say it was a funny kind of drama. But it was torture to me."

As Tom listened to her lament, he felt a deep compassion for this teen child/woman who was trapped in such a bizarre situation. The more she spoke, the more she resembled Jessica. Her facial expressions were the same, and so were her gestures. It was uncanny, and Tom felt as if he was looking at Jessica when she was much younger than he had ever known her. It was almost as if he was looking at the way she must have been before they had met. It gave him a peculiar feeling of having moved backwards in time. He tried to say something but it sounded ridiculous. Instead of words, he held Linda's face in his hands and wiped her tears. Then he gently pulled her head down onto his shoulder, still caressing her. Linda felt an overwhelming sense of relief as she rested in his arms.

"Jessica," Tom said, "I believed that Jessica was in you since you were four years old."

"Why didn't you tell me?" Linda said with a sigh. She felt surrendered in Tom's arms.

"I hadn't the courage to say it loudly."

"Tom, you were brave before--when we were married. You always said what you believed. That was one of the reasons I loved you. What happened to you?" She rubbed his chest just as Jessica used to do. "You're not as I remember you from before I died . . . I mean, before I changed my body. What changed you?"

"Jessica, I don't know," Tom said, lost in deep thought. "Maybe after Jessica's death, I mean your death

. . . whatever . . . I was very depressed. I felt very lonely and lost my ambition in life."

Linda held Tom's hand and kissed it. She looked in his eyes and said, "What did you think about me? Tell me the truth."

"Well, as I said, you always had Jessica's image in you." He smiled slightly as Linda rubbed his chest and neck tenderly. It was the most pleasant sensation he had felt in a very long while.

"I liked to watch you talking like her, eating like her, laughing like her. The only difference was the age. You are more impulsive than Jessica. But I didn't know how Jessica was when she was your age."

"What about Angela? Did she believe the same as you did?"

"I think so."

"So nobody dared to talk about it," Linda said, almost to herself. "What a pity!" Linda lay down and pulled Tom nearer to her. "Come, Tom, lie beside me," she whispered.

"Jessica, please, I don't want to complicate the situation even more for all of us."

"I don't understand what you mean, Tom," Linda said, holding him in her arms. "Don't be afraid. Relax and don't think of Angela. She's in a deep sleep right now. I heard her snoring."

"All right, I'll do what you want," Tom said, hugging her. "The situation is already so mixed up."

"Since I died. Right?"

"Right," Tom said, closing his eyes and kissing her with passion. He felt with every fiber of his being that he was kissing Jessica. He blotted out the memory of Angela, the woman whom he had also loved for fourteen years, and who was his wife. He blotted out the knowledge that the girl in his arms was also--at least in the eyes of the world--his stepdaughter, and had barely reached her mid-teens.

"I wanted to feel that I was still alive, like nothing had happened to me," Linda said as she started to undo his shirt buttons. "Do you see what I mean, Tom dear?"

Linda's fingers were massaging his chest, just like Jessica used to do when she wanted to express her desires before she made love. Tom held Linda's head and started to kiss her again, madly whispering, "Oh Jessica, I missed you, I love you . . ."

* * *

The next morning was Saturday. Angela was busying herself around the house when she noticed that it was eleven o'clock and Linda had not yet come down. She called up to her, and received a sleepy acknowledgement from Linda.

About fifteen minutes later, when Linda did make an appearance downstairs, she still seemed sleepy.

"Did you get to sleep last night?" Angela asked.

"Why do you ask?" Linda replied in a tone that conveyed her lack of interest in the question.

"You mean you don't know whether you slept or not? It seems as if you must have been up very late."

"I don't know." Linda said.

Linda looked at Angela's face, trying to read her thoughts. What was she seeing?

"What are you thinking, Angela?"

"Oh, nothing. Did you take your sleeping pill?"

"No. I didn't. I was very tired and it was late. So I thought I could sleep easily. What about you, Angela? Did you take a pill?"

"No, I was sleepy before I went up. I don't know what was wrong with me yesterday. I was tired but relaxed in a way. So I didn't feel I needed any help in getting to sleep."

Linda was satisfied to hear that. It meant that Angela hadn't detected the presence of the sleeping pill in her tea.

"Maybe it was because you were working hard in the garden yesterday," Linda said, trying to find an acceptable explanation that might allay any puzzlement Angela had about why she had felt sleepy.

"No, I don't think so. I wasn't even out in the garden. It was rainy, remember?"

"Yeah, you're right," Linda said. "Where's Tom?"

"Still asleep, I think, just like you were."

"What? Is he sick or something?" Linda wanted to go upstairs immediately to wake him, but she checked herself.

"No. Maybe he was working too late," Angela said. Then she looked directly into Linda's eyes, like she wanted to see the truth, and said, "Did you say goodnight to Tom?"

Linda felt a tremor of fear. It seemed as if Angela suspected that something had happened between her and Tom. But Linda kept cool. She was certain that Angela had not seen them together, so let her have her suspicions.

"No, I didn't say goodnight to him because we were both late, so I said good morning instead." Even as she said it she realized this was a provocative answer, but she didn't care. It was even fun to torment Angela a bit.

"Aha! I see," Angela said.

"What do you mean?"

"Nothing, nothing."

Linda decided to change the subject. "I decided to accompany you to the lecture," she said.

"Oh, so Tom told you about it."

"Yes, he told me. But why did you want to keep me away from it? Do you think you're the one who decides what's good or bad for me?"

This time she was spoiling for a quarrel, and didn't mind if Angela knew it.

"Yes, I think so," Angela responded coolly. "I am your mother and I--"

"No, Angela, you are not my mother. Don't even think that you bore me for nine months in your womb. It was only few hours, the time between my death and my birth. That's all."

"All right Linda, that's enough. I don't want to discuss it or argue with you."

"First of all, don't call me Linda. I've told you a hundred times." Linda was raising her voice and it had acquired an angry, rasping edge.

"I don't think you have any more right to hearing this lecture than I have. I'm the one who is a victim of reincarnation. You just happened to be the medium for this misfortune. Sister!"

Angela covered her face with her hands and cried loudly.

"I am sorry," Linda said. She turned around and walked briskly up the stairs.

Angela went on sobbing. Her heart was in torment. She guessed what had happened that last night. When she woke up in the morning she had smelled Linda's special perfume in their bed. And there were no words for the agony of soul that now afflicted her. What would become of them all now?

= CHAPTER 9 =

Dr. Karl Ruben, Professor of Parapsychology at the University of Philadelphia was giving his lecture in the Hotel Marriott. The title of the lecture was "Reincarnation, reality and fantasy." There were a couple of hundred people in attendance, of all ages. Dr. Rubens was a stout man of about sixty, and he lectured in a booming voice that had a trace of a foreign accent, and which seemed to carry some authority. He had had a lifelong interest in paranormal psychology, he said, and his findings were the result of much research and reflection. The audience was quiet and attentive. Occasionally a ripple of laughter would go around the group as the professor told an amusing anecdote, but generally the atmosphere was serious.

Tom, Angela and Linda sat together about halfway back from the podium. Angela had wanted to sit at the back of the room so they could leave if the lecture was boring, but Tom wanted to get closer to the speaker. It was also Tom who had insisted on taking Linda with them. Angela had put up a fight. She argued it might be unwise or even harmful for Linda to hear the lecture, but Tom was determined that Linda should come, as was Linda herself. Linda was fully aware of Angela's resistance, and the drive down to the hotel was tense-- Linda found that often now she was feeling anger at Angela, sometimes for no real reason. For her part, Angela had almost given up hope of ever living a normal life again. But she made an effort not to resent Linda, and to ignore her suspicions about Linda and Tom. The truth was that Angela did not think her mental stability could withstand the knowledge that her husband was having an affair with her daughter, who also claimed to be his former wife. So she tried to shut it out, although at some other level of her mind, she knew she had to know, one way or another.

Professor Ruben started with interesting statements about hypnotism. He then discussed some retrospective cases, in which people had undergone repeated sessions of hypnosis, to track them back to their childhood. Some of these subjects could trace their way back to their very first day of life. They could describe how painful the labor was for their mother, and how disturbing it was for them to be forced out of their warm place of rest. Other subjects could under hypnosis go one step further back to what they believed was a previous life. They could describe who they were, when and where.

Tom was transfixed by this information, which matched what he had been reading for himself. Even Angela found it interesting, but she was skeptical of hypnosis.

At the end of the lecture Professor Ruben was ready to take some questions from the audience. Linda looked to Tom and Angela; both seemed to have no intention of participating in the discussion. So Linda suddenly raised her hand. Angela pulled Linda's hand down and kept it down. Linda struggled to free her hand, but Angela's grip was firm. She did not want Linda embarrassing them all with whatever question she had in mind.

But Linda was not to be so easily restrained. She raised the other hand. Angela saw this and gritted her teeth. However, she was not prepared to cause a public scene, so this time she tried some gentle persuasion. The Professor was busy answering someone else, and Angela whispered to Linda, "Don't ask any questions, please. Let's go now."

Linda looked to Tom. Tom was listening to the Professor and made no move to leave. Linda was upset by Angela's interference and decided that nothing was going to stop her from doing what she wanted. She stood up and stepped across Angela and reached the aisle. Angela gave a scarcely audible sigh and muttered, "Oh, no."

Linda walked down to the front of the room until she reached the first row, where she waited for the Professor to acknowledge her.

Professor Ruben noticed her immediately and smiled at her. When he finished answering one questioner he turned to Linda. "Yes, young lady?" he said, beaming.

"Professor can I ask you something?" Linda took a step nearer the podium.

"Of course, you may ask whatever you want," Ruben said softly.

"Are you yourself reincarnated?" Linda asked.

A ripple of amusement went through the audience, and Professor Ruben had a big smile on his face. But Linda wasn't smiling. She turned back and looked at the audience with a serious expression on her face, as if to say, what are you laughing at?

Professor Ruben then understood that this exceptionally poised young woman was not trying to make a joke, so he altered his expression accordingly. Now he was serious again, although a faint smile played around the corners of his mouth.

"No, I am not reincarnated, Miss…?"

Linda was not about to supply him with her name. "Professor, have you ever seen, even once in your life, one person at least, who was a reincarnation of someone else?"

"No, I don't think so, not personally, but I--"

"You don't think, Professor, or you didn't think?" Linda said in a sharp tone, which made even his faint smile disappear.

Tom and Angela were beginning to squirm in their seats. What was Linda doing? They would have given anything to be out of that lecture room and on their way home.

"What do you want to say, miss…" Ruben began, but again Linda cut him off, her voice confident and strong, belying her youth.

"Had all your patients undergone hypnosis treatment?" she asked.

"Yes, all of them. But what is it that you're trying to say?" He was obviously becoming a little irritated.

"How can you be certain of what you were telling us now about reincarnation if you relied entirely on hypnotized patients?"

"Hypnotism today is a well established medical tool in the treatment of psychic patients."

Ruben had reassumed his professorial manner, but Linda was not impressed.

"Professor, please, you base your conclusions basically on psychic patients sleeping in trances, isn't that right?" Linda said, and then glanced around her at the audience. Everyone had gone quiet, wondering who on earth this young girl was.

"Yes, but--"

"Do you really know what a reincarnated person is? He's the one who can tell you, without hypnosis, how he lived before, who he or she was. He's the one who remembers how difficult it was as a child to start talking. He knew that he had the ability to speak and he understood every word that people uttered around him; but his tongue felt paralyzed, so he could not say what he wanted to say. He could tell you how difficult it was to stand up straight on his feet and then fall down like a crippled person. Do you really understand what he feels?"

Linda was speaking without a pause. She didn't give Professor Ruben a chance to say a word. He just stood there, letting her continue; it was clear that he was as astonished as everyone else by Linda's impassioned outburst. And she wasn't finished yet.

"When he grows up," she continued, "he may find himself surrounded by his relatives and friends, those he knew in his previous life, and recall all the memories and experiences that he had then. But he can't tell anybody about his situation, because he's afraid of being considered crazy."

"And how would you know all of these things? Have you been reading about them?"

Professor Ruben finally managed to get a word in. He was plainly annoyed at Linda's refusal to acknowledge him as the expert that he believed himself to be.

Linda did not answer his question directly. "Can you imagine what it is like being a reincarnated soul?" she continued. "When you come back to this life born, say, as the son to your wife, who has married a friend from your past life? Imagine what a hell you would experience because you cannot communicate this to anyone. Do you think that's amusing or it is a misfortune?"

Professor Ruben had recovered his dignified manner and did not respond to Linda's provocative remark. Instead, he had a question of his own. "I am curious, are you yourself reincarnated?" He said it with a smile, as if to encourage Linda to respond.

Tom held his breath for a moment. He had no idea what Linda was about to say. He feared that she would say exactly what she believed about herself and perhaps even point out Tom and Angela in the audience, so everyone would know who she was talking about. He did not put anything past Linda, because he was just beginning to grasp what torment she had lived through. And he remembered how strong-willed Jessica was also. Once she decided to do something, she just went ahead and did it, often without thought for the consequences.

As it turned out, Linda was not about to divulge everything about her personal history.

"Professor," she said, with irritation in her voice, "don't try to analyze or hypnotize me. I am not one of your psychic patients. At the beginning of your lecture, you said that reincarnation is a very interesting subject. I'm telling you it's not an interesting subject; it's merely a curse. Every reincarnated person is cursed all his life."

With that, Linda turned abruptly and made her way quickly to the exit. She did not look at either Tom or Angela. A buzz went up among the audience, but Professor Ruben just stood in silence. It appeared that he was not pleased to be upstaged by a fourteen-year- old girl. Tom and Angela quickly got up from their seats and made their way out of the hotel. They caught up with Linda in the hotel foyer. No one spoke, and the drive home was also endured in silence.

When they got home it was almost midnight. Tom said he wanted to do a little more work before going to bed. He also wanted time to digest the events of the evening. He was more than ever convinced that reincarnation was a reality, and for the first time he felt that he could understand it and accept it without going through so much mental anguish. Why it had happened he still didn't know, but the fact that it had now settled into his mind simply as part of the reality of things.

Angela was not so sanguine. In fact, she was furious. She was seething with anger over Linda's behavior, which she thought was extremely rude — the way she had spoken to the professor without showing any respect, the way she had called attention to herself and made a spectacle of herself, the way she had insisted on questioning the professor when Angela had specifically asked her not to and had even tried to physically restrain her. It was all too much.

As for Linda, she felt a certain degree of exhilaration at what she had accomplished, although she kept quiet because she knew that Angela was mad at her and maybe Tom also. But she had shown everyone that she had a mind of her own, and she had also shown that pompous professor that he didn't know half as much as he thought he did. That had certainly felt good!

Linda went to her bedroom straightaway. There was a parcel that had come for her in the mail that day, and she hadn't yet had a chance to open it. She knew exactly what was in it; she had ordered it on the Internet a week ago. She tore open the parcel, slit the inner wrapping, and gazed down at the contents. It was perfect! It was the one thing that had been missing. She picked the item up and stroked it gently, up and down. It felt sleek and soft. Then she sat down in front of her dressing-table. She took the precious item and arranged it according to the purpose for which it was designed. She gazed into her mirror with awe and delight. The long red wig fitted perfectly. The flaming tresses that she had so loved when they had hung on her when she was Jessica had been restored. The hair flowed down across her shoulders and down her back. It was luxurious. The color was perfect. It was an exact match. As she looked into the mirror, she felt that she was finally, after all these lonely, estranging years, looking at herself, not at an impostor. She had no words to describe how wonderful that made her feels.

At that moment she heard footsteps approaching her door. Then there was a firm knock. Linda did not reply. She knew who it was. Tom did not knock like that--his knock was softer. The knock came again, more insistent this time.

"Linda!" announced Angela's voice. "I need to talk to you. I know you're in there."

Again, Linda made no reply.

Angela did not wait. She couldn't hold her feelings in anymore. She wanted to tell Linda exactly what she thought of her behavior. It was her responsibility to do so, she thought, since Tom obviously had no intention of doing it.

Angela turned the door knob and entered the room. Linda turned around to face her, and Angela stopped dead in her tracks, her mouth open. She was speechless. It was as if she was seeing her dead sister again.

Linda smiled at her. "Hello," she said.

"Linda, what are you doing?"

"Do you like it?'

"Look, Linda, your behavior tonight was

unacceptable..."

"Why? Am I not allowed to ask Mr. Big Shot a question?"

"It was the way you did it, you--"

"Well, I'm sorry I didn't do it the way you think I should, but I don't see what gives you the right--"

"Because I'm your mother, that's why!"

"Oh, please." Linda turned back to face the mirror, her back to Angela.

"Don't you turn your back on me. And get that ridiculous thing off your head."

Linda saw in the mirror Angela approaching her from behind. Angela suddenly reached out and pulled the wig from Linda's head. Linda screamed and shouted, "No!" as Angela went to toss it into the trash can in the corner of the room. Linda leapt up, whirled around and lunged at Angela. The wig flew across the room as Linda thudded into Angela's body. The force of the girl's lunge knocked Angela backwards and off her feet. She landed in an undignified heap on the floor. Her face reddening, she scrambled up immediately, coming face to face with Linda, who had been going to retrieve the wig but was blocked by Angela's body. Angela pulled her arm back and slapped Linda hard across the face. Linda squealed and grimaced, and in a spontaneous reaction to being attacked, tried to slap Angela back. Angela parried the blow with her arm and for a few moments the two pushed and wrestled each other, before Angela again lost her footing and fell to the floor, with Linda toppling down on top of her with her fingers at Angela's throat.

At that moment the door flew open and Tom rushed in. He had heard the commotion from downstairs and had run up to see what on earth was going on.

"Oh, my God," he muttered to himself as he rushed towards the two struggling bodies. He took hold of Linda's arms and using all his strength pulled her off Angela.

"What the hell are you doing?" He yelled at Linda, shaking her.

"Leave me alone!" she yelled back. "It was her fault."

Angela had got to her feet, and was rubbing her throat. "She tried to kill me!" she shouted at Tom.

"No, I did not," Linda yelled back. She turned to Tom. "She shouldn't have touched my hair."

"It's not your hair, it's just a stupid wig," said Angela, who was still breathing heavily.

"What are you talking about?" said Tom.

Linda had gone across to the other side of the room to pick up the wig, that lay in a crumpled heap on the floor. She smoothed it out and held it in her hands. She didn't quite have the nerve to put it on her head again, as she felt that Angela was in a hysterical mood and there was no telling how she would react.

Tom took one look at the wig and did not need anyone to explain what the quarrel had been about. He looked at Angela and saw some ugly red blotches beginning to form around her neck where Linda had grabbed her. He felt sorry for her. She looked so beaten, so scared.

"Don't do that ever again," he said to Linda sternly.

"What me?" Linda exclaimed, incredulous. "What about her? She slapped me. She started it! Are you taking her side? I can't believe this."

"I'm not taking anyone's side. I just don't want anything like this to happen again. OK?"

Linda went silent. She didn't want to alienate Tom.

Angela was still struggling to regain her dignity. She said nothing either, but simply walked out of the room, just brushing by Linda's arm as she did so. Linda tensed up but managed to control herself. She wanted to cry.

I think you better go to bed," said Tom. He felt a kind of weariness that he had not experienced for quite some time. His earlier feelings of tranquility and acceptance were nowhere to be found.

= CHAPTER 10 =

Two days had passed since the violent quarrel. The atmosphere in the house was tense, to say the least. Linda and Angela kept apart from each other as much as possible. Linda felt more than ever resolved to pursue her plan to secure Tom's affections and not let them go. If Angela tried to intervene, then it would be all the worse for her.

Now she sat in Dr. Johnson's treatment room again. She mustn't run out of those sleeping pills, since they had been working well for her. Working well for Angela, that is. She thought of Dr. Johnson as kindly but foolish, and had no doubt that she could manipulate him to get what she wanted.

"Well, Doc, I took the pill but didn't feel a thing. I mean I didn't sleep well. Then I took another one, which helped me to fall asleep, but then I woke up again after few hours. Then I couldn't sleep anymore."

"Linda, it is strange to hear that, because the effect of the tablets lasts almost eight hours or more. How could you wake up after two hours? That's very unusual."

"I think I need something stronger, doctor, or maybe I need to take two pills at a time? Do you think that would help?"

"No, no Linda! Never take two pills at a time. One tablet is enough for an adult."

"But Doc, what would happen if I took two?"

"No, that would be double the usual adult dose. I don't know how I can help you. All the other sleeping pills I know are bitter. And you refuse to take anything with a bitter taste, is that correct?"

"Yes. I can't swallow any bitter medicine at all. I may vomit immediately."

"The pills you have are the only ones which are almost tasteless."

"Then give me the same pills again."

"What, did you take all the pills I gave you?"

"Yes, doctor. You gave me those pills nine days ago, and now I only have two left. Please give me more. I don't have time to come every week."

"All right, I'll write you a prescription to be repeated two times."

"Thank you, doctor. I must say I didn't feel anything of the side effects that are described on the slip. No headache, nothing!

"I'm glad to hear that, but if it doesn't help I have to remit you to Dr. White."

"Who is this?"

"He is a psychiatrist."

"A psychiatrist? Why? What do you think, doctor? You think I'm a crazy psychopath or something?"

"No Linda, of course not, I wanted to have his opinion about the best medicine for you."

"Why? Don't you know every medicine, Doctor?"

"Yes, of course, but Dr White has more experience in such cases like yours."

"What cases? You mean crazy people?"

"No, no."

Dr. Johnson smiled, but showed no willingness to placate her further. What he was not telling Linda was that the previous day Angela had called him and explained again about Linda's "fixation," as she put it, on Jessica. She had urged Dr. Johnson to refer Linda to a psychiatrist. Dr. Johnson was not sure he took Angela very seriously, and from his observations, Linda looked like a rather normal teenager, albeit one with a sleeping problem. But he had agreed nonetheless that if the problem continued, he would arrange for her to see Dr. White.

* * *

"I don't know what's the matter with me, Tom."

"What is it, Angela? Do you feel sick or something?"

"No, I don't feel any pain or fever, but I feel sleepy all day long."

"Maybe you need some exercise. You don't go out working in the garden so much nowadays."

"I don't have any interest in it anymore. I only want to sleep."

"Why don't you try going to the gym? It's not far from here. You can also swim there, too." Tom said.

"That's a good idea. I haven't swum for ages. Would you come with me?"

"Me? Oh no! I don't have time. When I get home from several of those client meetings, one straight after another, I'm already exhausted. Take Linda with you. I mean Jessica!" He reproached himself immediately. Whatever name he called her was wrong. If he called her Linda, he would please Angela, but then his whole being would scream out, No, she's Jessica! But if he called her Jessica, he knew that Angela would react badly.

This time Angela was silent. She looked at Tom and turned her head quickly away, thinking of Linda's perfume in Tom's clothes. But so far she could not muster the courage to challenge him.

For several days, the three of them slipped into an uneasy routine. Every evening Linda was anxious to make coffee for Tom and Angela by herself. She would put one sleeping tablet in Angela's tea. Every night, Angela felt sleepy early and left Tom in his study while she went up to bed. Half an hour later Linda would put on her make-up and her sexiest nightgown, and of course her beloved wig, the thing that made the transformation complete. Then she was ready to meet her beloved "husband," Tom. After a while with him in his study, she would leave him alone so that he could finish his work. Then she would wait, excited and expectant, until he came up to her. This was exactly how it had been in their marriage. It was almost as if she hadn't died.

Tom always left the light and his computer on in the study. That was his precaution in case Angela woke up and came downstairs for drink or a snack. She never interfered with Tom when he was working, so she wouldn't even look inside the study.

Tom knew nothing of what Linda was doing with Angela. So when he came into Linda's room at night he was never relaxed. He was thinking that Angela might suddenly come into the room or that she would hear them talking--or worse. As for Linda, she was not prepared to take him into her confidence. She just said that she was sure Angela would not wake up the entire night.

"You know, Jessica," Tom said on one of these nights, "I wonder why Angela is so tired every day. She doesn't even do any physical work that would explain it. Maybe she's sick or something?"

"I don't know, maybe you're right." Linda said. "Are you worried about her?"

"Of course, aren't you?" Tom asked.

"Yes of course, she's my sister!"

"Jessica!" Tom said, his voice showing disapproval.

"Don't you worry about me," Linda said, "I am your actual wife. Did you forget?"

"I don't know, Jessica. To me you are Jessica, the one who I loved so intensely, and at the same time you are like my daughter."

"Daughter? Please, Tom, don't say that again. I am nobody's daughter. Even when I was a child I didn't feel that Angela was my mother. Don't you see?" She got closer to him on the bed. "Relax, my darling, and take off your shirt. Let me help you."

The following day, when Linda came back from school, Angela wasn't downstairs as she usually was. Linda shouted, "Anybody home? Angela! Are you upstairs?"

When there was no reply she assumed that Angela was out shopping. She entered the kitchen and opened the refrigerator, aiming to fix herself something to eat. She was just about to pull some bread and jam out when she heard a thudding sound coming from upstairs. She suddenly felt afraid, remembering that there had recently been a rash of burglaries in the neighborhood. Was there an intruder in the house?

"Who's there?" Linda shouted nervously. "Angela, are you there?"

When she didn't hear an answer, she ran to the phone to call the police. But as she picked up the receiver she heard Angela's voice calling from upstairs.

"I'm here," she said, her voice sounding faint.

Linda hurried upstairs and found Angela still in bed.

"Angela. Are you still asleep? What's going on? Are you sick? What was that thumping sound I heard?"

"Oh, that was nothing. I just dropped a couple of books on the floor. I've been in bed most of the day. After breakfast I felt tired, so I went back to sleep. I don't know why I'm so tired. What time is it now?"

"It's after four. Do you feel any pain or anything?" Linda asked.

"No!"

"Did you take your sleeping pill yesterday?"

"No, no."

"Shall I make a cup of coffee for you to wake you up?"

"No, I don't like coffee."

"I'll fix some food for you then," Linda said. "Don't worry. You have to wake up. Take a shower. How can you sleep tonight if you are still in bed now? So, what do you want to eat?"

Linda prepared a quick, light salad, which was all Angela had asked for.

There seemed to be at least a temporary truce between the two of them. Linda was careful not to upset Angela, and for her part Angela avoided making any provocative remarks.

* * *

When Tom came home at about seven, he said hi to Linda, who was in her room studying, and then went downstairs, where Angela was in the sitting room, reading.

"How are you, today, Angela?" Tom asked.

"I slept until four today, can you imagine?"

"I know, Jessica told me," Tom said.

"So, she told you," Angela said.

"Yes."

"What more did she tell you?"

"Nothing. Why?"

"I'm just wondering." Angela said. She had not been able to concentrate on her book and had begun brooding about her situation, not only regarding Linda but also about her health. She had always been fairly robust, physically, and it was very unusual for her to be as tired as this, without any apparent cause.

"What do you mean?" Tom said.

"Nothing, Tom. I think I should go to the doctor for a checkup."

"O.K. When are you going?" Tom asked.

"I don't know. I haven't called them yet."

"Yeah, I think that's a good idea," Tom said.

* * *

Later that evening, Linda went downstairs to ask Tom if he wanted his coffee.

"Yes, Jessica thanks," Tom replied.

"What about you, Angela? Some tea?" Linda asked."I don't know. Every time I drink tea, I feel sleepy. Strange! Don't you think so Tom?" Angela said.

"Are you joking, Angela?" Linda said.

"No, I'm not joking."

"Maybe you've became tolerant to tea," Linda said. Seeing Angela's puzzled look she quickly added, "Just joking. Would you like a cup of cocoa then?"

"No, thanks. I think I'll have some coffee."

"I thought you said earlier you didn't like coffee?"

"Normally I don't, but I fancy some now."

Having seen Angela very sleepy the whole day, Linda decided to ease off on her game of trickery. She didn't want to overdo it at the moment. So for once Angela got nothing more than she asked for--just an ordinary cup of coffee. And it worked the way coffee normally does.

"Tom, I think I feel better," Angela said after a few minutes. "I'm not so sleepy."

"Maybe you should drink more coffee," said Tom. "Or maybe it's because you slept the whole day, so you're waking up now."

"Maybe," Angela said. "I don't know what the answer is. I just don't want to be so tired anymore."

"At any rate, call Dr Johnson tomorrow and make an appointment," Tom said.

"O.K. I'll do that. I hope I can sleep tonight."

Since she was feeling a bit better, Angela decided not to go upstairs early as she had done for the last few days. Tom was still working in his study, while Linda was in her room holding a book in her hands, but not reading a word of it. She was waiting for Angela to go upstairs to bed. She hadn't bargained on Angela being so stimulated by the coffee that she would stay downstairs all this time.

After a while Linda got restless and went down to say goodnight to Tom and to check on Angela. She went directly to Tom in the study, and noticed that Angela had followed her. Angela stood in the doorway.

"I don't want to interfere Tom, I just want to say goodnight." Linda said, trying to sound casual and fighting back her irritation with Angela.

"Good night, Jessica!" Tom smiled at her but his attention was focused on the silent figure standing in the doorway.

"Now you can kiss Tom goodnight," Angela said, looking directly at Linda. Her tone was neutral but Linda knew what was behind it. As did Tom, especially when Angela turned to look at him, an expression of bitterness on her face.

For a moment there was a tense silence as Tom and Linda wondered whether another flare-up was imminent. But before anyone said anything else, Angela turned around and walked off.

Linda tried not to pay any attention to Angela's unwelcome interruption. She embraced Tom and kissed him, but only for a minute or two. Then she went back up to her room. She guessed that Angela wouldn't be going to bed for a while, so she decided to let this night go without adventure.

Almost in spite of herself, she felt a twinge of compassion for Angela. She argued with herself about it. Maybe she didn't want to hurt Angela's feelings. Angela was her sister, after all. Linda lay on her bed remembering how nicely the two of them had lived together in her previous life. But it hurt her when she saw that Angela didn't care for her feelings now. Then Linda remembered how they had always competed with each other, and that a layer of jealousy had never been far below the surface. And now, in this strangest of all situations, Angela had taken her husband. It felt to Linda as if Angela had stolen Tom. But then she thought again-- all right, Angela didn't know for certain about Jessica's reincarnation as Linda. She might still be trying to hold on to the belief that Linda was really her daughter, not her sister. Perhaps the truth was too frightening for her to accept. Then Linda wondered why Angela reacted so badly when she saw her and Tom showing affection to each other. What was wrong with sharing a kiss? What did Angela expect--a handshake? Linda thought it was very strange and selfish of Angela to react like that, as if she was the only one who was allowed to kiss Tom. But then she felt that she needed to have patience with Angela, since she was her sister after all.

So Linda's mind went back and forth, and she tossed around for an hour or so before falling asleep.

* * *

The next day, when Tom came home in the late afternoon, the first thing he asked Angela was about the result of her visit to Dr. Johnson.

"Well, he said everything is O.K.," Angela said. "He called me half an hour ago to tell me that the blood examination was normal."

"That's it? Nothing else? What about your sleeping the whole day?"

"He couldn't explain it," Angela said. "He asked me if I took my sleeping pills more than one at a time. But I explained to him that I didn't even touch the pills last week, because I didn't need them. I was sleepy before I even finished my tea."

"What did he say?" Tom asked.

"He didn't believe that I wasn't taking the pills."

"Angela, is it possible you were taking the pills unconsciously, without even knowing it."

"Tom, please, not you too. I'm not crazy," Angela said, laughing.

"All right, I believe you. How did you feel today?"

"Very good so far. I went out shopping and thought that I might go to the gym sometime," Angela said.

"Good idea, Angela, very good!"

"Would you like to come with me?"

"I told you I couldn't. But why don't you take Jessica with you?"

When she heard the name "Jessica," she sighed and shook her head and looked at Tom with bitterness. "I don't think she will come with me when you're home. She wants to be with you."

She spoke very deliberately, and it was clear to Tom what she was implying. She sounded jealous.

Neither spoke for a few seconds. Then Angela continued, and now her tone was openly taunting, "By the way, I bought Linda a perfume spray just like mine. Give it to her and tell her to use it when she kisses you." She spat out the last words with some force.

"What? What's going on?" Tom was surprised by the sudden change in Angela's demeanor.

"Oh Tom, come on! I smell her perfume very strongly on your clothes and in our bed. Do you think I'm stupid? Do you think I'm blind? Do you--"

"Angela, please--stop."

Angela glared at him. Her eyes reddened and filled with tears. Then she collapsed on the couch, crying loudly.

Tom went across to comfort her, but she fought him off, screaming, "Get away from me!" Then she jumped up from the couch and ran off upstairs, sobbing,

"Oh God! What have I done? Why me?"

Tom sat down with his head in his hands. He was worried not only about Angela's health but also her mental stability. But what could he do? He couldn't break the bond he felt with Linda/Jessica--it went back too far and extended too deep. And he also was forced to admit to himself that he wanted Linda physically, much more so than he wanted Angela, his legal wife. Yet he knew that this would break, indeed was breaking, Angela's heart. And Angela had done nothing wrong, nothing to deserve this. They had been quite happy together until all this came along.

= CHAPTER 11 =

After about an hour, Angela came back downstairs. She appeared to have regained control of herself, which was a relief to Tom. As he sat and watched TV, she went to the kitchen to prepare some sandwiches and tea.

When Linda heard Angela moving around in the kitchen, she went down from her room to see what she was doing. She saw the tea was already prepared.

"I feel a bit hungry," Linda said.

"Do you want my sandwich?"

"No thanks, I'd like to eat something else."

Both Angela and Linda were determined to be polite to each other, however much of a strain it caused.

Angela started eating, while Linda went back up to her room. She put a sleeping pill in her pocket and came down again.

"I see you changed your clothes, Angela. Are you going out?"

"Yes, I'm going to the gym."

"Oh really? That's good."

"Would you like to come with me?"

"No, I can't. I have a test tomorrow."

"Really? You didn't mention it."

Angela heard Tom say something to her from the sitting room, but she couldn't hear him properly. "What did you say Tom?" she asked, and took her sandwich to the sitting room.

The moment Angela left the kitchen, Linda took out the pill from her pocket and threw it in the teapot and stirred the tea vigorously.

When Angela returned to fetch the tea, Linda was upstairs with a bowl of cereal and milk.

Angela poured the tea in her cup and added sugar. She stayed in the kitchen eating, and then drank a second cup of tea. Then she took her sports-bag and left the house without saying goodbye to either of them. She was thinking of what would happen between Tom and Linda when she was away. Ugly pictures formed in her mind and she couldn't drive them away. She was very bitter about the situation.

Linda was watching from her window and saw Angela driving away. She hurried to finish her make-up. After a few minutes, Tom knocked gently on the door and entered immediately.

Linda was naked to the waist, sitting facing her mirror, occupied with her make-up.

"Oh Tom, you scared me!" she exclaimed, looking up at his reflection in the mirror and making no attempt to cover up.

"Sorry! Jessica. I think Angela knows about us more than we thought. She gave me this perfume to give to you."

Linda spun round in her swivel chair and took the spray bottle from Tom. He gazed down at her breasts.

"Oh no," she said as she examined the bottle. "Not this spray. I hate it. It's like hers."

"That's right."

"But why? She knows I don't like it."

"She complained that she can smell your perfume all over--in our bed, even in my clothes."

Linda shrugged her bare shoulders. "What's the big deal? It's my right to kiss you and make love to you, whenever I want to. What do you say, Tom?"

"Jessica please, you have to understand that we are not married as in your past life. We are not alone as before."

"What are you trying to say, Tom? Do you mean that my sister is your wife and I am out?"

"I mean, we can't openly say that we are in love with each other."

"Aren't we, Tom?"

"No. Yes. No, even if we are, you are only thirteen years old!"

"No--fourteen. Next month."

"Fourteen or seventeen, it still doesn't work. The fact is that you are still a minor until you turn eighteen. Legally, I can't have a sexual relationship with you because you're still under eighteen. Don't you see?"

"What are you saying? Do you think that I'm going to wait four more years before I can marry you?

"Yes, Jessica. I believe so. We have to," Tom said.

Linda's lips curled into a pout. "Look, I've already waited fourteen years," she said, making her impatience clear. "I knew that my body wasn't in an adult form and I was afraid to say that I love you or I wanted to make love to you. You might have laughed at me."

She stood up, pulling her shoulders back and trying to emphasize her still-growing breasts. She knew the power that a woman's breasts could have over a man.

Tom's mouth went dry. Already Linda's breasts reminded him of Jessica's. He wanted to grab her and kiss her all over, but he restrained himself. Linda was continuing to speak: "But now I feel mature enough to tell anybody how I feel about you. Isn't my body now almost as mature as Angela's? Don't you think so? Now, I can face Angela without fear. I will tell her that I still love my husband and I am his real wife, not she."

Tom shook his head. He felt as if a great weight was descending on his shoulders. But before he could say anything, Linda put her arms softly around his neck and kissed him.

"Jessica, please listen to me carefully," Tom said, trying to free himself from her arms. "If anybody discovers that I am having a sexual relationship with you, I may be accused of sexual child abuse and I'd go to jail."

"Why, Tom?" Linda was slightly alarmed. "Why is it a crime to love somebody? I don't understand."

Tom sat down on the bed, and Linda sat next to him, still clad only in her skirt. She was not prepared for the obstacles that were now being placed in their path, and she was not sure how to react.

"Because you aren't eighteen years old yet," Tom said emphatically. "Nobody would understand nor believe the situation we are in right now. And it's against the law."

"And what do you suggest I shall do, Mr. Law?" Linda said. She had no patience at all with what the law said regarding love. What had law got to do with matters of the heart? She continued, "Keep my mouth shut and wait an additional four long years? Sleeping alone like a child?"

"That's what you're going to have to do if you want to keep us from scandal," Tom said earnestly, "and me from jail."

Linda was frightened to hear that. "I don't want you to suffer because of me," she said. "You know how much I love you. But I can't tolerate how Angela's acting like the first lady of this house. *Our* house, Tom!"

"What do you want her to do? Disappear or kill herself? She's got every right to be here. I am married to her, after all. And she has already suffered from the day you were born."

"Sorry that I was born again." Linda's eyes reddened and she turned away from Tom. "It is my fault then."

"Nobody's fault, Jessica," he said softly, reaching out for her and putting his arm around her shoulders. "That's not what I meant. She's already--"

Linda turned back to face him. "She took advantage of the situation by taking you away from me. That's it." Linda was angry now. "She was always competing with me."

"No, Jessica, no. That's not what happened. She and I were both desperate and lonely. We both thought you were dead, you must understand that."

"So since you were both desperate and lonely, you kind of complemented each other, I suppose."

"You were the link that united us together."

"So, I was the reason you married her. What am I supposed to do now, kill myself?"

"Please, Jessica be reasonable," Tom held her arms, trying to persuade her. It was as much as he could do to stop himself from caressing her breasts. "We must keep our relationship secret for four more years at least. There's no other alternative."

"What about Angela?"

"What about her?"

"I mean, do you intend to continue living with her as before? Do you still love her?"

"I can't say I ever loved her. But she was the only person that reminded me of you, Jessica."

"When you made love to her, did you think of me too, Tom?" Linda was raising her voice, insistent, wanting an answer.

Tom was embarrassed. He didn't want to think of making love to Angela while he was inflamed with desire for Linda. So he just deflected the question. "What do you want me to do now, Jessica?"

"I don't want anything. I only want you back," Linda sobbed. "I want my life back. That's all Tom, don't you see? Is that so much to ask?"

"What do you suggest, tell Angela about us?"

"Yes, tell her the truth," Linda said while wiping her tears, "if you love me more than her."

"Jessica, don't you still love your sister as you used to do before?"

"Not exactly. I feel that she betrayed me by taking you away from me."

"But Angela didn't take me away from you," Tom said. "You're very obsessed with this idea. I have her to thank for accepting my invitation to stay with me and marry me after your death. I was very lonely. Everything around me reminded me of you. I remembered you in every corner of this house. I couldn't bear to be staying here alone. I was going crazy. So I had to escape from my memories. She was the only one who understood me and felt your loss as well. She suffered more from your death than from her own husband's death. Did you realize that?"

Linda didn't realize that, and had not even thought about it. But she didn't want to dwell on it. All she knew was that Angela was a threat to her love for Tom, and Tom seemed to be taking Angela's part in all this. She felt hurt. She decided to press Tom further.

"Do you still feel lonely? Or do you feel that I'm back? Do you still want Angela to fill my place? Do you, Tom?" she asked, edging closer to Tom on the bed.

"I don't know what I should do, Jessica," Tom said. "Please put yourself in my position or hers. What's the solution? I don't know. It's a dilemma."

"I don't know what to do either. But put yourself in my position," Linda argued softly. "I only know one thing. I wanted you for myself alone. That's all I wanted, darling. And it's all I still want. Try to understand." She lay back on the bed, and then continued, "Come over here next to me and relax. Let's try to find a solution."

Tom's resistance was weakening. Linda was too seductive, too alluring, for him to ignore. Just like Jessica had been. He took off his shirt and lay down next to her on her bed. Linda embraced him and let her face rest on his neck, like Jessica used to do all those years before.

Linda started to take unzip her skirt. Tom didn't move. He was looking at the ceiling.

"Jessica!" he hissed. "Angela may return any time now."

Linda didn't comment.

"I said Angela might come," Tom repeated.

"Let her come," Linda said angrily. "Why are you so afraid of her?"

Impatiently she sat up, pulled her gown on and walked out of the room. "I need a glass of water," she said. Tom heard her go downstairs. This was typical Jessica. She was so volatile and unpredictable. Her mood would change in a moment. Tom grabbed his shirt and followed her downstairs.

Suddenly, the phone rang and Tom grabbed it. After giving his usual greeting, "Hi, this is Tom," he heard a female voice saying,

"Is this Mr. Tom Wells?"

"Yes, who are you?" Tom asked.

"I'm calling from the Emergency room. Your wife was transported from the gym. There was an accident in the pool. She nearly drowned."

"What?" Tom shouted, "Is she all right?"
"She's in a coma."

= CHAPTER 12 =

Tom and Linda sat in the waiting hall nearby the intensive care ward. It was nearly nine o'clock in the evening. After an hour or so, a nurse came out to tell them that Angela was still in a coma. Tom asked to talk to the doctor in charge.

When the doctor came, Linda anxiously asked: "How is she?"

"She is all right," said the doctor, a young man with a harassed look on his face. "I mean, she is still in coma, but her condition has stabilized. I think that it won't take a long time until she recovers her consciousness."

Tom asked, "Are you sure that she'll recover without brain damage? How long will it take until she returns to consciousness?"

"Look, I said she'll be all right," the doctor said, in a kind and calm voice that showed their concerns had registered with him. "She'll wake up. But when, I don't know. Any complications? I don't know. But so far every thing is all right."

"Can I see her, doctor?" Tom asked.

"Yes, doctor can we see her?" Linda repeated.

"I'm sorry you can't now. But we'll call on you as soon as she wakes up."

Tom nodded. Taking Linda by the hand he turned around and headed for the exit. There was no point in hanging around longer. But his mind was full of questions.

After leaving the hospital Tom drove straight to the gym where the accident had happened. Although it was late, there was a chance that someone would still be there.

"I want to know what happened," he said to Linda. "I'll ask the people in the gym, how could she nearly drown when she knows how to swim? Angela's a good swimmer."

Linda had been sitting in the passenger seat without saying a word. She was lost in her own thoughts. She had an explanation for the accident. She suspected that it might have been the effect of the pills. But she was certainly not going to share that information with Tom. After all, the doctor said that Angela would recover, so there would be no permanent harm done. Linda struggled to avoid the feelings of guilt that were beginning to tug at her.

"What do you think?" Tom asked. "I mean, how can somebody drown in a swimming pool? To me, that's a mystery."

Again, Linda kept silent. Tom assumed that Linda was worried about Angela and that was why she had gone quiet. He felt quite relieved at that--it showed that in spite of the situation, Linda still cared for Angela, her mother.

"Don't worry," Tom said to reassure Linda, "the doctor said it's going to be O.K. You heard him."

"I'm not worried. Would you react the same way if it was me in a coma?"

"Of course."

Now it was Tom's turn to go silent.

When they reached the gym, there were still lights on. At the reception desk, a man named Mark greeted them with a tired smile. Tom explained who they were, and asked Mark, "May I know how it happened?"

"We don't know exactly what happened," Mark said. "Rick called me to help him. We tried to resuscitate her by pumping out as much water from her lungs as we could. Then we gave her artificial respiration. In the meantime the ambulance came and the medical team took over."

"Who is Rick?"

Mark picked up his walkie-talkie and called Rick to come to the reception.

"Rick was the lifeguard on duty at the time of the accident," Mark said.

When Rick emerged from one of the back rooms, Tom asked him, "Can you tell me what happened exactly?"

"Well," said Rick, who was a big man in his mid-twenties with long blond hair, "I was watching some kids playing on the other side of the pool. They were making a lot of noise. You know kids. Then suddenly I heard somebody screaming for help."

"You mean Angela?"

"No, someone else. It was an old man sitting on the side of the pool. When I looked in the direction he was pointing, I saw her under the water surface motionless. So I jumped in the pool. We pulled her out and started to--"

"Did anybody tell you how this happened?" Tom asked.

"Yeah, the old man told me later that she was climbing the ladder out of the pool, but she was doing it very slowly. It seemed like she was too tired or too weak to get the whole way up. She might have fainted as she was climbing. I don't know. I don't think she'd been in the pool for all that long. How is she now?"

"I don't know, she's still in coma."

Rick nodded sympathetically, and looked from Tom to Linda.

Linda had been standing at Tom's side listening silently without asking questions or saying a word. But she was pretty sure she knew what had happened and why.

When Tom and Linda arrived at home, it was nearly midnight. Tom called the hospital and asked about Angela's condition. She was still in coma.

Tom sat down in his study, nervous and agitated. He felt helpless. Linda went upstairs to change clothes, and then came back down again.

"Tom, would you like to drink or eat something?"

"No, thanks."

"You haven't eaten anything for ages. You must be hungry."

"No, I don't feel hungry," Tom said.

"Something to drink then…"

"No, thanks."

"What's the matter with you? Are you angry with me?"

"No, no. Why should I--"

"Then what's the matter, are you worried?"

"Of course I am. Angela's in a coma! How could I not be worried?"

"The doctor said that there's nothing to worry about."

"He didn't exactly say that. And he didn't say how long she'll stay in this coma. And he didn't say or know what permanent damage she might suffer."

"What damage are you talking about?"

Tom sighed. "She could get a permanent brain damage, for example. She may become paralyzed, unable to walk or talk. I don't know. I'm not a doctor."

"But he didn't mention anything like that."

"Ah, you don't know how doctors try to calm the family. As long as there's no evident complication, they don't mention it. But when they discover something wrong, they'll say, something like that was expected in such cases."

"Tom, whatever happens, you can't prevent complications in Angela's condition by sitting here worrying and getting hungry. Come on; help me fix something to eat.

"Linda, I told you, I'm not hungry. I have no appetite."

"It's Jessica!" Linda screamed at him.

Tom gave an exasperated wave of his hand. "I mean Jessica. I'm sorry. I'm upset and tired."

"Well, I'm going to fix some food, and I think you should eat some of it."

They had a late night snack, which they ate mostly in silence. Afterwards, Tom called the hospital again. There was no change in Angela's condition. She was still in coma. Tom hung up the phone and looked at Linda.

"It wasn't wise of me to let her go to the gym alone."

"But Tom! How could you have known that this would happen? She was normal yesterday and today, and Dr. Johnson didn't find any disease either."

"I think she was sick. Did she tell you about anything abnormal that she was experiencing? Other than tiredness?" Tom asked.

"No she didn't mention anything. She doesn't tell me anyhow."

Linda went over to Tom and put her arm around his shoulders. "Aren't you tired, Tom? I know you are. Come, let's go up. We need to get some sleep."

"I want to stay here for a while, but you can go and sleep."

"All right. I'll go before you and take a shower. But don't sit here all night calling the hospital every five minutes. There's no point."

She embraced Tom and kissed him. He hardly responded. He was so worried about Angela that it all but extinguished his desire for Linda.

After the shower Linda went to the master bedroom, took off her gown, and lay in Angela's bed waiting for Tom to come. Thoughts rushed through her mind thick and fast. She loved this experience of being alone with Tom. And she was going to be sleeping with him in the same bed. How long she had waited for this! It felt as if she was just beginning to live as she had done in her former existence, and this was what she longed for. Nothing else mattered.

She was genuinely worried about Angela, but she liked the fact that Angela wasn't around. She hoped that Angela would soon wake up from her coma, and there wouldn't be any complications.

But subconsciously she wished that Angela would stay as long as possible in the hospital. It was an ideal solution, although she knew in her heart that it could only be temporary. Angela would in all likelihood be home soon and the same old situation would return.

When Tom finally abandoned his lonely vigil in his study and slipped under the bedcovers next to Linda, he was nervous. His mind was occupied not only with Angela's condition but also with what he knew were Linda's ambitions. He thought of what the future might hold for him, and for all three of them. He realized that for the next four years, Linda's sexual impulsiveness and jealousy would always be a threat to him. She could put him in a critical situation. If Angela found out, he could be at Angela's mercy. She could take revenge on him and he could be sent to jail for what he was doing with Linda.

He was also troubled by the fact that in a way he was relieved that Angela was in the hospital. It meant that the situation was eased. He could live with Linda as before, talking freely, joking and sleeping with her. He always enjoyed every moment he spent with her and felt as if his previous life with Jessica had been restored, almost as if the interruption of thirteen years had never happened. But the shadow of Angela's presence between them was always there, bringing him back to reality. He was torn between these two women. He couldn't just abandon Angela. He felt compassion for her. She had always been there when he needed her. She was a perfect companion. She helped him through the period of depression that had darkened his life after Jessica's death. She took care of everything concerning their daily life. She always offered to do his things before hers. Now, he couldn't just leave her alone, even in four years time, when Linda turned eighteen. He couldn't be so mean to her. He had to find a way of including her in his plans for the future. But he had no idea of how to do that.

Then other thoughts rushed in. He was deeply fond of Angela, but he had to admit that he loved Jessica more than anybody else. Everything reminded him of her since the day she died. He couldn't stop thinking of Jessica. She was always there. In all these years he hadn't forgotten her, and he didn't think it would have been any different had Jessica not reappeared as Linda. As he lay next to Linda, he recalled all those incidents over the years, and how he had come to believe that Jessica had returned: When Linda was only four; he had realized that Jessica was in her, but he couldn't say it out loud. His belief hadn't wavered in nine years. Now he was anxious to see Jessica mature again. Once more she was filling his life, even though she bore the image of Linda, the teenage girl whose gentle breathing he could hear and whose warm flesh he could feel as they lay silently together. Whenever he talked to Linda, he heard the voice of Jessica. Whenever he held her, he felt like Jessica was in his arms. But he was filled with regret and anguish that now Jessica was back, and rapidly maturing into the woman he had known, he couldn't possess as he had done before. It all had to be in secret, as if it was somehow illegitimate. They could not love in the broad light of day. Now Tom felt that the three of them were joined together in something that resembled a Greek tragedy: he was afflicted, torn between two women who loved him; Jessica had lived a tortured life since the day of her birth, and Angela knew everything and was suffering too.

He couldn't sleep.

* * *

Next morning, Tom and Linda were waiting outside the intensive care ward for the doctor. The door opened and a nurse came out.

"Hi, how is she?" Tom stood up and asked.

"Sorry, who do you mean?" the nurse said.

"My wife, Angela…"

"I don't know, I'll call the doctor…"

The nurse returned to the intensive care ward. Tom looked at Linda and she looked back at him.

"What's going on here? I don't…" Tom said annoyed.

"Nobody knows a thing." Linda said.

A doctor came out, the same young man they had spoken to the previous day.

"Are you Tom?" the doctor asked.

"Yes, how is Angela…" Tom asked.

"She's all right. She opened her eyes. And we've been able to communicate with her. But she's still very weak, so…"

"Are there any complications?"

"It's all looking good at the moment."

Tom suddenly felt like crying, but he held his emotions in. "Doctor, please, we must see her," he said.

"It's O.K., but only for a few minutes. And don't talk to her. That might disturb her."

Tom's heart was wrenched when he saw his wife lying in the hospital bed, weak and pale. Her eyes were closed, and the nurse thought she was just sleeping.

Linda looked down at her sister and her rival. She felt so many things she didn't know what she felt. She couldn't deny that she felt guilty. But nor could she deny that she hoped Angela's recovery was not all that fast. She had Tom now, and Angela couldn't do a thing about it.

* * *

During the days of her convalescence, Angela's health improved quickly. Linda visited her every day and did what she could to help. She still felt guilty. She went out of her way to be kind. She made sure she didn't argue with Angela like she used to do at home. Every day Linda would stay with Angela in the afternoon, until Tom came later. Then after a while Linda would accompany him home.

Linda was very satisfied, since she was able to spend the rest of the evenings and the nights alone with Tom in one bed. It was no longer Angela's and Tom's bed. It was Jessica's and Tom's.

Tom couldn't deny that he was satisfied too. He fancied that Jessica was still alive and they were together again as man and wife.

It was Angela who was suffering. Every time Tom left her, accompanied by Linda, she suspected that something wrong was going on. Her intuition told her that Tom and Linda were having an intimate relationship. It was just something about the way they related to each other. You could tell. But Angela had no way of proving it, and nor did she dare to. If she had proof, what could she do about it without bringing chaos and heartbreak to all three lives? What should she do?

She lay awake for hours in her hospital bed, reviewing every possible angle to the situation. She loved Tom and she didn't want to lose him. Linda was her daughter, and in spite of the almost unbearable tensions of the last few weeks, she loved her. She loved her sister

Jessica too, although she still couldn't bring herself to acknowledge that Linda was a reincarnation of Jessica. She knew that if she hurt Linda she would hurt Tom too.

Day and night the dilemma continued. Angela was in a miserable situation, caught between two people who were both dear to her. She couldn't live without them and yet she couldn't tolerate seeing them live as lovers in front of her eyes. Oh God! What a hell!

Pretty soon, Angela decided that she couldn't tolerate any longer the stream of thoughts and fears that she was torturing herself with. She felt as if she was going crazy. She must leave the hospital as soon as possible. So, instead of just lying there and being depressed and uncooperative, she resolved to eat all the food they offered her (even if, like hospital food everywhere, it was awful), take her medicines regularly and do her physical exercises without complaint. She simply decided to act as if her condition was improving. All that was to impress the doctors and nurses and convince them that she was making fast progress. She was hoping to be discharged soon.

Once Linda heard that Angela was recovering and might be discharged as early as the following week, she acted as if she was very pleased about the happy tidings. At the same time she was worried, and soon got close to panic. She needed to do some serious thinking. If she didn't do something, her dream life would soon come to an end. She would not have the same opportunity for at least four years. There would nowhere near as much intimate contact and unrestrained love with Tom as she had now. Angela would be back, exerting her right to be with Tom, to sleep with him, to be first in his life. Linda could not bear the thought. She thus decided to try the impossible--she must somehow keep Angela away from home a little longer. As long as Angela was not home, Tom would still be hers alone!

But what could she do? Linda thought for a while and came up with nothing. Then an idea flashed into her mind: Stick with what works! She had got what she wanted through the sleeping pill ruse, so why couldn't she do it again? It might be more difficult this time, since Angela was in the hospital, but Linda resolved to try. The pills hadn't really harmed Angela before, Linda thought, and maybe she would have fallen in the swimming pool anyway. Thus Linda silenced her conscience, while at the same time deciding that she would do whatever it took to keep Angela out of the picture, as far as she and Tom were concerned. Suddenly a dark thought came to her: Would you kill her if necessary? Linda beat back the question. She didn't want to answer it. But she did know that she wasn't going to let anyone--sister or no sister-- come between her and Tom.

For the moment, though, a simple strategy would be enough. If she could not put a pill in Angela's tea, she may try to put it in a fruit juice or even mix it with her soup. Nothing would happen to Angela, Linda reassured herself, trying hard to dismiss her darker thoughts. Angela was already in the hospital, and in the event that she needed help, she would get it immediately.

= CHAPTER 13 =

The next day, Linda was at the hospital as usual, visiting with Angela. When dinner was served, there was no way for Linda to put a pill in Angela's juice. She tried to convince Angela to have a cup of tea or coffee. But Angela said she didn't want any. Linda was getting nervous. She had to accomplish this somehow.

Angela noticed that Linda seemed edgy and abrupt, and she asked her about it. Linda made up some excuses about having a lot of schoolwork to do that evening and feeling the pressure. Finally, Angela got up and went to the bathroom. With a sigh of relief, Linda took the opportunity to put a pill in the juice bottle. Now she could relax. And she thought with a mischievous inner smile, soon Angela would be relaxing too! It almost seemed like fun.

Tom came later on as usual. Angela told him that she would be discharged in two or three days.

"That's great!" said Tom. "That means you have nothing to worry about."

He looked at her and smiled. Then he looked across at Linda, who was smiling too.

"All the blood examinations and the x-rays were normal," Angela said happily.

"Yeah, you look much better," Tom said. "Don't you feel it?"

"Yes, I do, Tom," Angela said.

She looked at them both and then looked away, thinking. Tom stood up and reached over for Angela's juice bottle to drink from it. Linda was quick to intervene.

"Don't drink from Angela's juice. She likes it and there's only one left. Take another one. Take this one." Linda took the bottle from him and handed him another sort of juice.

Angela and Tom were both surprised at Linda's concern for Angela's interests. Tom was pleased. Whenever there was any sign of good feeling between Linda and Angela, he found himself hoping that all the problems would just go away. Linda smiled and put Angela's juice back on her table.

* * *

Next morning, Angela was still sleeping when the nurse came in to check on her. Her blood pressure was too low, and Angela reacted sluggishly. The nurse reported her observations to the doctor.

During the doctor's morning visit, Angela tried to show some vitality--she had no idea why she didn't feel so lively today--but her pretense didn't fool the doctor.

"How do you feel today, Angela?"

"Very well doctor, I feel great!" Angela's speech was slightly slurred.

"Did you not get to sleep until late last night?" the doctor asked.

"No, doctor, I slept as usual." Angela tried to remember. "Or maybe it was earlier…I think."

"You need to do extra exercises," the doctor said, turning to the nurse, "with an extra stroll today."

"When are you going to release me, doctor?" Angela asked, still slurring her speech but unaware of it.

"Well, Angela, it may take some more days," the doctor said.

"What's going on doctor?"

"Your blood pressure is low. Don't worry, we'll manage."

"Do you think I'll be discharged soon, as planned, doctor?"

"I hope so, so far."

After school Linda came to visit. Angela told her about what happened during the morning.

"He told me that he's going to discharge me as planned. I was really relieved," Angela said, sounding well satisfied. "I was afraid they may keep me longer. I hate hospitals."

Linda's heart sank. So one pill wasn't strong enough, and Angela would soon be returning home. Linda knew she must act quickly, and guessed that nobody would suspect a sleeping pill--or two.

When Angela had to take her walk with the assistant nurse, Linda excused herself from joining them, saying she had to finish her schoolwork. As soon as they had left the room, Linda opened the fruit juice bottle that was at Angela's bedside and took a quick sip. Then she took two pills out of her pocket and put them in the juice bottle. She then shook it vigorously to dissolve the pills quickly. She opened the bottle to taste it, and didn't perceive any change in the taste of the juice. She was satisfied; she had done the job that she had been thinking of all day. And she did not feel guilty about doubling the dose. She had to do what she had to do, and that was all there was to it.

After a few minutes Linda joined Angela outside, telling her she couldn't concentrate on schoolwork sitting in that dull room alone.

When they returned Angela wanted to drink so Linda poured out a glass of juice for her. Linda enjoyed watching Angela drinking the cup to the end. She asked

Angela if she would like another cup. Angela declined. Linda, however, was certain that Angela would finish the bottle before she slept.

* * *

Next morning. Angela didn't seem to be able to wake up as she had been used to doing over the last few days. She couldn't eat breakfast and fell asleep again. She had no idea what was wrong, and felt alarmed by the sudden change. The nurse called the doctor who came immediately.

Every thing appeared normal except that Angela's blood pressure was very low. So the doctor ordered an injection to raise it. He also planned a new blood examination. He appointed a nurse to check Angela's blood pressure, pulse and temperature every fifteen minutes.

After a few hours' more sleep, Angela woke up and still seemed tired. The doctor checked her again and explained what he had done for her.

"As far I can see," the doctor added, "All tests we made were normal. I can't explain your weakness and sleepiness."

"Maybe it's because of the medicines I take," Angela uttered in a low, slurred voice.

"You get only vitamins and analeptics to keep you awake and restore your vitality."

"So you can't find out what's wrong with me, doctor?"

"No, I can't. There is nothing wrong that we can find."

"What about my blood pressure?" Angela asked. "Isn't that the reason I'm feeling sleepy?"

"I should say the contrary. Your low blood pressure is a result of your deep sleep. That's all."

"So, what you suggest then, doctor?" Angela said.

"May I suggest you consult our psychiatrist?" the doctor said, "I can talk to him and set up a time for him to examine you."

"What do you mean, doctor?" Angela reacted, her voice filled with dismay. "A psychiatrist? For what? You don't think that I'm crazy or something?"

"No, no, Angela. Don't take it personally." The doctor tried to calm her down. "I told you I checked everything but I couldn't find any organic disease as a cause for your condition. I therefore presumed that it could be a psychological or emotional condition that keeps you in this deep sleep for so long."

"Nonsense. I don't feel any thing's wrong with me mentally. I have no psychic or emotional…"

Angela didn't complete her sentence. She thought of Tom and Linda. Suddenly the thought crossed her mind that maybe the strain of that situation was what was causing her to be so sleepy. Maybe subconsciously she didn't want to go home and confront the situation all over again. So maybe the doctor might be right; the problem was psychological. Angela didn't want to look at the doctor. She kept silent and looked down at the bed covers.

"Shall I send him to you?" the doctor asked.

"As you want, doctor,"

Angela answered very faintly. She lay back in bed and closed her eyes in grief.

* * *

The next day, Linda was sitting in Dr. Johnson's office. She knew exactly what she wanted.

"Yes, Dr. Johnson, I've been sleeping better taking the pills. But now I need more."

"I don't like to give you more tablets."

"Why, doctor?"

"You may get addicted to them. No sleeping pills are without risk."

"But I need them," Linda pleaded. "Sometimes I can't sleep because I think too much about Angela, I mean my... mother. You know she's in the hospital."

"Yes, I know. How is she today?"

"She's doing well, I think."

"Well, I told you last time I would like to refer you to Dr. White, the psychiatrist."

But doctor, I don't need a psychiatrist. I only need some tablets. I promise I'll not take them regularly. Just when I need them."

Just as Linda had expected, she was able to manipulate Dr. Johnson into giving her what she wanted. He gave her another prescription and she went straight to the pharmacy.

* * *

The psychiatrist examined Angela the same day. She annoyed her with her fussy manner, but she answered all her questions as best she could. She reported that Angela did show some signs of stress trauma but there was no definite psychic disorder. She recommended that Angela should stop taking all medication, in order to rule out any unexpected side effects. She advised her to stay a few more days in the hospital.

Angela didn't like to hear that, though she unwillingly agreed to stay until the cause of her strange weakness could be discovered.

Linda had no idea of what had happened that morning. When she arrived Angela was not in her room. Linda wasted no time. She took out two tablets from her pocket and opened the juice bottle, which was on Angela's table.

At that very moment Angela and the nurse came in. Linda was holding the bottle in one hand and the tablets with the other hand. Her heart was pounding. Was she about to be caught red-handed? She smiled with difficulty, clamping her right hand, which held the tablets, into a fist.

"Oh there you are, Angela," she said, as casually as she could. "How are you today?"

"Thank you, I feel better today." Angela said.

"I like to taste this juice," Linda said, and took a cup and filled it.

Nothing in Angela's reaction suggested that she had noticed anything unusual. She immediately turned to the nurse and continued the discussion they had been having before they saw Linda.

Linda was not going to lose her nerve. Turning away from the other women so that they could not see her hands, and tossed a couple of tablets into the bottle and screwed the cap in place.

When the nurse left the room, Angela told Linda everything that had happened that day.

"So I am not taking vitamins," Angela added, "or any other medicines any more."

"But Angela, this is not right. You need vitamins."

"She, the psychiatrist, I mean, said that I have to see her twice weekly."

"What's going on Angela? What's wrong?"

"She says I need treatment for a supposed psychic trauma."

"What kind of trauma? Is it because of the accident in the pool?"

"That was like a trigger for my condition now," Angela said.

"I don't understand."

"Well, the pool incident was not the actual cause of my sleepiness."

"But?" Linda asked.

"The cause is something deeper than that."

"I don't get you, Angela."

"You don't understand that because you don't feel my suffering," Angela said, her eyes filling with tears.

"Linda . . . Jessica . . . you can ask Tom."

"But Angela--"

"I don't want to discuss it now. Please."

Angela turned her face away, sobbing silently. Linda quietly left the room. In spite of Angela's tears, Linda's heart had hardened towards her. She hoped that the combination of the pills and Angela's psychiatric treatment would keep her in the hospital for quite a while longer. Beyond that--well, she would cross that bridge when she came to it.

The following day, Angela was as weak as the day before. It was difficult for her to wake up. Her body felt like a heavy log, and she just wanted to lie in bed and never move. She was disoriented enough not to call for help to go to the bathroom.

She struggled up from her bed feeling dizzy and went swaying to the bathroom.

She sat in the bathtub thinking about this unexplainable loss of energy. The only thing that was different was that she hadn't taken vitamins, in accordance with the psychiatrist's instructions. But in her foggy mental state, she did not reach the obvious conclusion, that she should not stop taking the vitamins. Instead, she concluded the opposite. She remembered that she had also drunk a lot of orange juice, which contains vitamin C and other vitamins. Maybe she was exhausted because she had not eliminated vitamins completely. So she decided to cut out all fruit juices.

When Linda arrived, Angela was out with the assistant nurse making her daily walk. Without hesitation, Linda took out two tablets and put both in Angela's juice bottle. She was even tempted to put in three this time, but she restrained herself. She then went looking for Angela. When she located her, she didn't approach her, but hid behind a pillar, waiting until Angela entered her room.

After a few minutes Linda came in as if she had just arrived. She found Angela sitting in a chair, looking alert.

"Angela you look livelier today than yesterday," Linda said, surprised.

"Yes, I do feel better today," Angela replied. She had no intention of confiding in Linda that earlier in the day she had had no energy at all. She seemed to have recovered now, so she didn't want to think about those alarming few hours in the morning.

"So you didn't take any medicine?" asked Linda.

"No."

"Did you take your walk today?" Linda said.

"Yes. I've just come in."

"Good! How about something to drink?" Linda asked.

"I'm not thirsty. Thanks."

When Tom arrived, he noticed that Angela seemed lively.

"I think it won't be long before they discharge you," he said.

"I hope so, Tom. I hate this room. I hate hospitals," Angela said bitterly.

"I brought you some fruit," Tom said.

"Thanks. But I still have some here."

"Well, these are fresher."

"I didn't touch any fruit today."

"Why not?"

"I was thinking of the vitamins they contain. You know. The psychiatrist, since yesterday, stopped the medicines I was taking, including the vitamins."

"Oh, O.K. Do you want something else? Ice-cream?" Tom said.

"No Tom thanks. I don't want anything," Angela said. "You and Linda can drink or eat what you want."

"Well, I feel thirsty," Tom said.

"Take my juice, I didn't touch it," Angela said, indicating her bottle with a wave of her hand.

"But Angela, vitamins are not poisons," Linda said, with a laugh.

"I know that. But even though they're good, I don't want to sabotage the course of treatment," Angela said. "Linda, please pour out a cup of juice for Tom. And have one yourself too."

"No, no, not me. I don't want to drink that--it's yours," Linda said.

"But you drank some yesterday. Why don't you want it today? Come on, drink, both of you. I told you I'm off drink juices. I feel better and I am glad."

Linda felt trapped. If she didn't drink from that bottle Angela might suspect something. So she was going to have to do it. She took a paper cup and filled it with the juice. Then she took another bottle of juice, which didn't contain any sleeping stuff, and began to fill a cup for Tom. But Angela noticed what she was doing.

"Linda, ah... Jessica, why don't you give Tom the same juice you've got?" Angela said.

Linda looked at Tom and said, "I remembered that Tom likes the strawberry. Isn't it so, Tom?"

"I don't mind. Whatever you give me is O.K.," Tom said.

Linda gave Tom the cup full of strawberry juice and took the orange juice for herself. She sipped a very small amount and then intentionally shook the cup. Some drops fell on her jeans. She jumped up with the cup in her hand and went in the bathroom to dry out the juice stain. She poured the juice in the washing basin and filled the cup with water. Then, she returned to Angela's room with the cup in her hand.

* * *

Over the next few days, Angela felt normal again. Each day she was awake before the nurse came. She didn't feel dizzy and was not drowsy as she used to feel every morning.

Her doctor was impressed by her progress. He thought that it was probably due to the psychiatric treatment. The psychiatrist suggested that her recovery was due to the psychological effect of not taking medicines, which had given Angela a feeling of independence and wellness.

The doctors planned to discharge her the next day on one condition--that she must continue her psychotherapy.

Linda was not surprised when she heard the news from Angela. Since her trick with the sleeping pills had failed, she had expected the worst. She became depressed, but she acted as happy as she could. It was all a pretense, but Jessica had always been a good actress. Behind the happy smile, Linda was thinking hard about her next step. She wanted to be rid of Angela, and no longer cared much about how this was to be accomplished. It just had to look like an accident that was all.

Tom was also flung back into turmoil at the prospect of Angela's return. He felt completely divided within himself. He loved having Linda with him alone but he also liked having Angela around. It had not been comfortable for him to see his wife incapacitated in a hospital bed. But he was worried. He thought of all the precautions he and Linda would have to take, the secrets they would have to keep. He was afraid that it would not be long before Angela discovered them and knew everything. Especially because she had already her suspicions about their relationship. All he could think of to do was to act normally and show his complete satisfaction and happiness at Angela's return. He knew in his heart that this would not be enough.

For her part, Angela was eager to return, to get out of that hated hospital and be in her own environment again. She had also secretly resolved to be on the watch for both of them. She was not going to put up with the situation anymore. Something had to give. She wondered whether Linda and Tom would start meeting somewhere other than the house when she returned. Perhaps they would go to some horrid little motel somewhere. She considered hiring a private detective. But she rejected the idea because it would cost her a fortune that she couldn't afford. On top of that, it might not produce any satisfactory evidence.

* * *

The day that Angela was coming home, Linda started cleaning the master bedroom, where she had spent happy nights together with Tom.

She changed the sheets and washed the dirty ones. She collected all her belongings that she had been left scattered around the room. She opened the windows and left them open all day to drive away all traces of her perfume. And she resented every minute of her work. She felt as if she was being demoted--kicked out of her position of favor and replaced by a deadly rival.

When Tom came home with Angela, he was surprised by the extent of Linda's house cleaning. But he couldn't say a word about the excellent work.

Angela went directly upstairs to inspect the bedrooms that had always been at the center of her thoughts when she was alone in the hospital. She kept imagining Tom and Linda lying together in her bed, making love. The images in her mind tormented her.

When she entered the bedroom, she saw that everything had been put in order. This was not the way things used to be. Normally, Tom left everything lying around; he could never be bothered to put anything away. She used to do all the work in that respect.

Angela sat on her make-up chair and looked at the bed. Again she thought of Tom and Linda lying together there, and all the disgusting things that they must have done. She felt helpless and desperate. She covered her face with her hands and wept silently.

* * *

In the afternoon Angela kept her appointment with the Psychiatrist. She seemed satisfied with her progress, although of course she made no mention of the dark thoughts that were becoming an obsession for her. When she came back, she found that Tom was already home, earlier than usual. He and Linda were in the sitting room, chatting.

Angela went up to her bedroom. She found her bed untouched. Then she entered Linda's room. She found the bed was all rumpled up. She swiftly concluded that both of them had been here, making love. As she left the bedroom she felt as if she might explode at any time, but as she descended the stairs she pressed her lips together firmly and resolved to keep silent, at least for the time being. She preferred to wait.

Linda and Tom were watching TV when Angela returned to the sitting room. As she sat down on the couch, Angela said, "The psychiatrist today was very satisfied and urged me to come twice a week."

"That's great," Tom said, turning away from the screen to look at Angela. "When's your next appointment?"

"The day after tomorrow at five P.M."

"Five P.M.," Tom said, "Would you like me to give you a lift?"

"I don't want to steal your time," Angela said. "If you wait for me until the end of the session, that'll take a while."

"I meant I can give you a lift over there," Tom said. "You can then call me when you're finished. Then I'll come back and pick you up."

Angela was certain in her own mind of what this meant. Tom wanted to be sure that she be with the psychiatrist when he made love to Linda. He wanted to make sure that he had the time to do whatever he liked with Linda. And no doubt she was cooperating every bit of the way.

"Thank you, Tom," Angela said, sweetly. "It's nice of you to take care of me. But I don't really want to consume your precious time with this."

"No. Not at all," Tom said smiling. "I do it with pleasure."

* * *

When the day of Angela's appointment arrived, Tom took her to the clinic. They arrived ten minutes before the appointment. He waited until he saw Angela entering the clinic, and then waited five more minutes to be sure that she was not coming back for some reason. He then drove back home as fast as he could. Linda was there, impatiently waiting for Tom's return. When he came in he called to Linda joyfully. But she didn't hear him. She was taking a shower. Tom hurried upstairs to the bathroom, tore off his clothes quickly and entered the bathroom naked.

"Oh, you scared me, Tom," said Linda as she pulled him under the shower. Both were laughing happily.

$=$ CHAPTER 14 $=$

The truth was that Angela had no appointment with the psychiatrist that day. She entered the clinic and waited until Tom drove away. When the nurse asked for her name Angela explained that she made a mistake. She thought that she had an appointment. The nurse tried to help by offering to arrange an appointment the same day, between the other patients.

"Thanks, but no thanks." Angela said. "I would like to come some other time. There's no hurry."

She remained in the waiting room, acting like she was waiting for her husband to come back. She waited about fifteen minutes and then asked the receptionist to call a taxi.

About ten minutes later, Angela was in the taxi nearing her home. She stopped the taxi about two hundred yards from the house and walked the remaining distance. She would have to take a chance on someone seeing her from the window, but given what she expected was going on inside the house, that didn't seem very likely.

She walked up the driveway, stepping lightly so she wouldn't make a sound on the gravel. She opened the front door very quietly, and entered the house. The first thing that greeted her was the sound of Linda's giggling laughter from upstairs. Hardly daring to breathe, Angela made her way slowly up the stairs. Now she could hear Tom's voice too, and he was also laughing joyfully. He sounded like a young kid.

Angela was about to creep towards the bedroom when she realized that the sounds were coming from the bathroom. She took three or four steps and was directly outside the door. The door was slightly ajar. In the crack she could see two bodies through the transparent shower curtain. The larger male body was standing upright; the smaller female body was clinging on to him, her knees drawn up, and her arms around his neck. They were rocking back and forth. Their mouths were locked together. The laughing had been replaced by small grunts and moans.

She closed her eyes for a few seconds. For a moment, she felt as if she was going to vomit. Then she opened her eyes, now filled with tears, and looked again at the bathroom scene. Although she had guessed what she would find, the shock of actually seeing it was no less severe. She knew that her life was ruined. Nothing that happened now could ever remedy the damage already done. Bitter, black despair filled her, and a maddening rage.

Angela retreated from the bathroom and went straight to the bedroom. She rummaged around in the desk drawer, searching for Tom's pistol, even though she didn't know how to use it.

She had never wanted to learn anything about guns. But now she did, and in a hurry. She found the pistol at the back of the top drawer, but she quickly saw that it was locked. She tried to figure out how to unlock it. There wasn't much time to waste.

Angela knew that her life was coming to an end. All she could feel was blank, unreasoning fury. Her life was just one long tragedy. She had lost her first husband and now she had lost not only her daughter but her second husband as well. They had no right to treat her in this dirty way, she thought. What did she do to them that they would betray her in such a manner? Nothing was left for her to live for. Her family had been all the life she had, her own little world. Now she had nothing left to live for.

Angela succeeded in unlocking the pistol. Sitting on the floor of the bedroom where she and Tom had enjoyed many happy times, she put the gun to her head. A feeling of sheer emptiness gripped her. But as she was about to pull the trigger, she heard a loud, happy laugh coming from Tom and an answering laugh from Linda.

They must be laughing at how they had fooled her, she thought. Angela saw red. She had been wrong. There was something left worth living for. One last act.

Under her breath she snarled to herself, "Alright, I'll show you what right punishment is for those who deceive me."

She ran out of the bedroom, heading to the bathroom, and pushed the door wide open. Linda and Tom were still in the shower, fooling around, laughing. Angela pointed the pistol directly at them and closed her eyes. She pulled the trigger, and then pulled it again, and again, and again. She was screaming madly, wild sounds coming from her mouth that she would not have believed she was capable of.

Suddenly the gun stopped firing, even though Angela was still desperately pulling the trigger. Realizing that there were no bullets left in the gun, she threw the pistol into the shower and stormed out of the bathroom. She did not wait to see the results of her work.

Returning to the bedroom, she searched for her sleeping pills. She opened the bottle and emptied the contents into her mouth. Then she reached for a glass of water and swallowed every single tablet.

Angela threw herself on the bed. Then she thought again of Tom and Linda making love on it, and she felt it was dirty, disgusting. She couldn't bear to be on it or anywhere near it. She threw herself on the floor and closed her eyes. Now there was nothing more to do.

She didn't hear the screaming that was coming from the bathroom.

* * *

Two of the nine bullets hit Tom. One penetrated his thigh and the other one pierced his chest. Linda was not hit. Linda was screaming in panic, and Tom was afraid to open the shower door, as if the thin plastic plate would protect him.

When they heard no more bullets, Linda, shaking from head to foot, opened the shower door and ran to close the bathroom door. When she saw Tom was bleeding, she started screaming again. Tom shouted at Linda to help him with some towels. She brought him the towels and pressed them on his wounds.

" Go down and call for the ambulance," Tom said, breathing heavily but retaining his presence of mind.

"I'm afraid of Angela!" Linda cried out. "She'll shoot me!"

"She's already used all the bullets," Tom said, wincing in pain, and knowing that he had to get help quickly. The towels were already soaked in blood. "But be careful, she may have a knife or something. She's gone crazy."

Still terrified, Linda sneaked out of the bathroom, a towel draped around her body. She passed the dark bedroom where Angela was lying on the floor. Linda assumed that Angela was downstairs, and just as she was at the top of the staircase, she remembered the phone in the bedroom. Using that would be quicker.

She entered the room and headed directly to the phone, which was placed on the other side of the bed. She snatched up the receiver and dialed 911 and waited. She heard something moving in the room and her heart jumped. But she looked around and saw nothing.

"Please come quickly," she said when the dispatcher answered the phone. Her words came out in a rush. "My father was shot and he is bleeding very much. He may die."

Linda gave the address, and while she was talking a noise coming from somewhere in the room caught her attention. Out of the corner of her eye she saw something moving. She whirled around just in time to see Angela's head appear behind the other side of the bed. Angela was trying to sit up.

Linda screamed and dropped the telephone receiver. She was certain that Angela was going to try to kill her. She ran downstairs, even dropping the only towel that covered her body. She opened the front door and stood in front of the house waiting for the ambulance.

Angela had forced herself to sit up when she had heard Linda's voice. She had no strength left, although she would have strangled Linda with her bare hands had she been able to. How had Linda survived that hail of bullets, Angela wondered. All she could think of as she slumped back unconscious on the floor was that she wanted Linda dead.

Tom sat on the floor with both hands on his wounds to stop the bleeding. He was focusing on staying conscious. He had to stay conscious. He prayed that Linda had been able to make the 911 call.

The paramedic team arrived within a few minutes. They raced up the stairs and took care of Tom. They managed to stop the bleeding and then carried Tom into the ambulance. Next they found Angela lying on the floor in coma. Her face was bluish gray and congested with whitish froth coming from her mouth. Her respiration was very shallow and laborious.

Linda stood behind the rescue team looking at Angela nervously, half-expecting her to jump up and try to continue her rampage.

One of the paramedics saw the empty bottle of pills on the floor near Angela.

"Are these hers, do you know?" one of them asked Linda.

"I don't know, I suppose they are, yes."

At the sound of Linda's voice, Angela opened her congested eyes and looked askance at Linda. Then she whispered harshly, "I'll be back, Jessica..."

The rescue team put Angela beside Tom in the ambulance and raced off at high speed to the hospital.

* * *

Linda was stunned. She didn't know what to do. No one had bothered to take care of her. After the ambulance left she hung around on the front porch, looking at the small knot of curious people who had gathered outside and were staring at her. She couldn't at first bring herself to return inside the house.

When she finally did so, she threw herself on the sofa and remained silent and motionless, as if she was afraid to move.

The police arrived. Linda told the two officers that she didn't know why her mother had tried to shoot them both. The officers seemed to be suspicious until she mentioned that Angela had been under psychiatric care. Whatever happened, Linda was determined that the secret she shared with Tom would remain a secret. She remembered what Tom had told her about what the consequences would be for him if they were discovered. But would Angela recover and tell? Linda prayed that she wouldn't.

The police car took her to the hospital. Linda had insisted that the officers take her there so she could find out how Tom was. And her mother too, of course, she added quickly.

As she rode in the back of the car, Linda beat back the worry she felt about Tom. She was sure he would be O.K. but she felt pretty numb about everything else. She would never have dreamed that Angela was capable of something like that.

Linda tried to think back over all the events of the last few days. She couldn't see that she had done anything wrong, or anything that she should regret. She considered the sleeping pills she had put in Angela's tea and juices. But she didn't see anything wrong to be ashamed of. That had merely been a defensive action aimed at regaining her previous position as Jessica, which was hers by right. She was only trying to get her man and her life back. But Angela wouldn't understand or accept that, Linda thought. Angela wanted to keep everything that Linda had possessed in her first life, even Tom. That was not fair.

Linda had no sympathy with Angela. Maybe Angela had felt insecure because of the affection that Tom was showing Linda. But nothing that had happened was sufficient reason to go crazy like that and try to kill them both. I'm her sister, Linda thought, can't she see that? Then Linda remembered how Angela was kind of jealous, always competing with her. Linda was not in the mood to acknowledge that she had been competitive too, and jealous on occasions. She reassured herself that all she had done was put sleeping pills in Angela's drinks-- they hadn't done any harm. She had made sure that Angela wouldn't be poisoned or dies of an overdose. She'd given her a dose just enough to keep her asleep, and out of her way. That was all. Of course Linda loved Angela. She had always loved her sister. It was only when Angela played the role of mother that Linda hated her.

As the police car drew up to the Emergency Room, Linda suddenly remembered Angela's warning. She was scared. She felt as if she could hear Angela's harsh voice again saying, "I'll be back, Jessica."

* * *

During the next few days Linda had a very hard time. Angela was still in a deep coma. Her condition worsened and her death was expected at any time. Linda's feelings were mixed. She did not want her sister to die. But equally she did not want her to wake up and tell her story.

The news about Tom was better. He was recovering after a complicated operation on his chest. It would take a while but he was expected to make a full recovery. The bullet had missed his heart by a fraction of an inch.

Linda visited both Tom and Angela every day. It seemed as if she was almost living in the hospital. Later, she did not know how she had got through those terrible days. But somehow she managed to stay strong.

After a week or so Angela's condition deteriorated rapidly. She died while Linda was at her bedside. Her passing was quiet, since she had never regained consciousness. At the moment of her death, as Linda waited for the next breath that would never come, Linda thought she saw Angela looking askance at her. It was an eerie moment, and Linda shut it out of her mind immediately.

* * *

At the inquest into Angela's death, the verdict was suicide. It was noted that Angela had had psychological problems, had recently been hospitalized, and had been depressed. The police closed their file on the case. There was no further investigation into why Angela had gone on her murderous assault. Tom and Linda felt hugely relieved, although the news of Angela's death had hit Tom hard. He wished with all his heart that things had not ended this way.

At Angela's funeral, Linda was one of only a few people in attendance. Linda felt lonely, and she found herself trembling. She was afraid of looking at the simple wooden coffin that contained the remains of the woman who had been her sister.

Tom was not present. He had been advised by his doctors to stay in the hospital because of his delicate condition following the serious operation. Linda wished he was there. It would make all the difference.

Just before the coffin was lowered into the earth, an ambulance arrived. Linda looked up to see Tom emerging from the ambulance, helped by a nurse.

Linda ran to Tom, feeling some relief at his arrival.

"She was my wife and I had to be here," Tom said.

The ceremony was short. Tom threw his flowers that the nurse was carrying for him onto the lid of the coffin. Linda moved forward, ready to throw her flowers too. Just then she felt a cold breeze sneaking through her clothes, chilling her body. She was surprised, as it was quite a warm day.

Then she turned back, suddenly afraid. Dismissing her fear as silly, she turned again and threw her flowers down onto the coffin. But then a strong gust of wind came from nowhere and blew hard against her, scattering the flowers and pushing her backward. She heard Angela's voice ringing around the cemetery:"I'll be back, Jessica!"

Terrified, Linda retreated a few steps. Then her knees gave way she fell to the ground. The nurse and Tom ran to her.

After a few seconds everything grew dark in her mind and she fell unconscious.

Tom and the nurse and the others carried her to the ambulance and laid her down on the stretcher. Tom sat near her holding her hand, comforting her.

"Tom," she whispered, her consciousness returning. "I feel something strange inside my belly. I think I am pregnant."

Just then both of them heard a ringing voice, familiar to them both, calling out in a tone that sent chills down their spines:

"I will be back!"

TRUST PUBLISHING

EMAIL: TRUSTPUBCO@GMAIL.COM